Look for other *SHOW STRIDES* books:

#2 Confidence Comeback

#3 Moving Up & Moving On

#4 Testing Friendships

#5 Packer Pressure

1
· SHOW STRIDES ·

School Horses & Show Ponies

Series created
by
Rennie Dyball

Published by
**The
Plaid Horse**

MAP OF
QUINCE OAKS

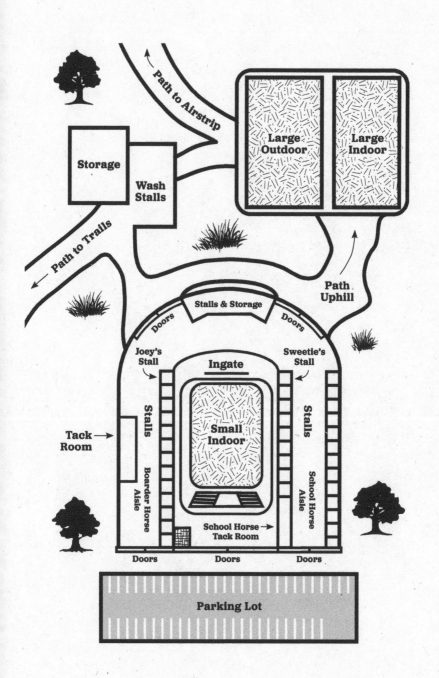

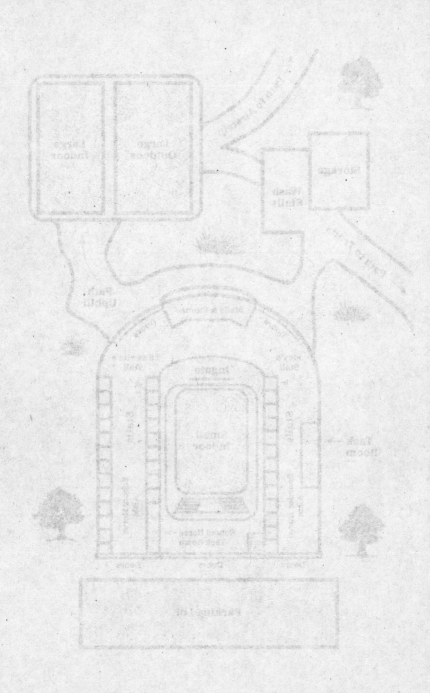

· CHAPTER 1 ·

Something inside the bright blue grooming box caught Tally's eye. Tucked in between a rubber currycomb and a hoof pick was a sheet of lined paper with a note scribbled on it in marker.

That's weird, Tally thought. *Why would someone at the barn write to me?* She bent down to pick up the paper, her new tall boots cutting into the back of her knees. Tally winced—a couple of her older barn friends had talked about how painful it can be to break in new tall boots, but she thought they were being a little overdramatic. Until now.

She unfolded the piece of notebook paper to find the following written inside in black Sharpie:

HARD WORK BEATS TALENT WHEN TALENT DOESN'T WORK HARD.

Dad, she thought immediately. No one else she knew would write in all capital letters like that. Plus, her dad was super proud of how much work she put into her riding. He was always sharing things he'd read about sports and athletes, encouraging her to follow their lead. "Tally up the ribbons!" he liked to say about horse shows. It was a cheesy play on her nickname (everyone had called her Tally—short for Natalia—for as long as she could remember), but she secretly loved when he said it. Who didn't love horse show ribbons? She scanned the paper again, the words blending together a bit in front of her eyes. Was her father trying to say she had talent or worked hard? Both? Not enough of either?

"Tally Hart!" A loud voice broke the silence of the tack room and startled Tally so much that she popped straight up, bumping her head on one of the school saddles mounted on the wall rack above her. In the doorway to the tack room, her instructor, Meg, laughed. Tally felt her cheeks turn red.

"Hey, I want to talk to you about the show coming up," said Meg.

"The show on the twenty-fourth, right? My parents

are dropping me off for the whole day," Tally said of the barn's upcoming schooling show, the fourth in a series of six. At the end of the series there would be an awards banquet and, rumor had it, super-long and fancy ribbons—longer than champion and reserve ribbons, even—awarded to first through sixth place for cumulative points over the show series. In two of the shows so far, Tally had gotten to ride Sweet Talker, a little chestnut Thoroughbred cross in her barn's lesson program. She'd never ridden in a series before.

"Great," Meg said. "Keep going with the hunter division you've been doing, but I also want you to do the medal class with Sweetie. I think you're ready."

Tally felt her heart thud excitedly in her chest. She'd watched the Quince Oaks junior equitation medal class at the last show and thought it looked like a blast. There was a rollback turn and a trot jump—a much more sophisticated course than the usual outside-diagonal-outside-diagonal pattern of the hunter trips.

"Sign up for that one too when you register, okay?" Meg reached for the buzzing phone in a pocket of her jeans.

"Thank you, Meg!" Tally called after her. Her
instructor gave her a thumbs-up as she walked down
the aisle, already talking on her phone, and Tally felt
that familiar swell of pride.

Tally practically skipped out of the tack room to go
celebrate the good news with Sweetie. Quince Oaks
(or Oaks for short, as the riders called it) was situated at the end of a long gravel driveway off a windy,
woodsy road. The Oaks barn was shaped like a
horseshoe—the right side was reserved for the lesson
program, which housed nearly thirty school horses
in stalls on either side of the aisle, with a tack room
on the open end by the barn entrance and parking
lot. The left side of the barn was designated for the
fifteen boarders' horses (the stalls were slightly bigger on the boarder side), and in the middle of the
horseshoe was one of the farm's two indoor rings that
everyone shared. From the parking lot, you looked
directly into that small indoor when the doors were
pushed open on their tracks. The top of the barn that
curved around the indoor ring had a few more stalls
that were used to store feed and supplies.

To get to the bigger indoor ring, you walked out

the far end of either aisle where the barn curved, and then up a hill. That's where Oaks horse shows were held. There was also a large outdoor ring right by the big indoor, plus a few miles of paths in the woods for trail riding.

Tally had ridden at Oaks for five years, and she would spend every single day there if she could. It was a unique place to ride due to its strong lesson program, in addition to the top-notch facilities that appealed to boarders. But she had to settle for just three days a week: once a week she took a lesson that her parents paid for, another day after school she was scheduled for a working-student shift, and on the third day she took the lesson that she earned from her shift. Technically, she was too young to be a working student, a position reserved for the teenagers at the barn. Even though Tally had just turned twelve, the barn manager, Brenna, had agreed to give her an unofficial junior working student position to earn her second lesson each week. Tally's gig didn't really seem much like work, since she had so much fun being around the horses and her barn friends. It was good exercise though, as she regularly fed the horses and ponies their hay, filled water buckets, cleaned tack and sometimes mucked stalls when the full-time grooms needed a hand.

Making her way down the aisle, Tally said hi to some of her favorite horses. Half of the school horses had stalls on the inside of the aisle. Those stalls were secured with mesh stall guards or a chain covered in rubber, so the horses could stick their necks out to watch what was going on around the barn. The horses on the outside of the aisle had sliding doors and a big window that opened up to the outside of the barn. Tally always thought those horses were the lucky ones, so when she rode an inside-aisle horse in one of her lessons, she'd spend extra time with it outdoors, walking or hand-grazing, since those horses didn't get to look outside nearly as often.

As she approached the end of the aisle, Tally saw Sweetie pin her ears at Harry, the horse in the next stall over.

"Oh, don't be grumpy, my girl," Tally told her softly as she approached. Sweetie acted like a typical mare on the ground, with strong opinions about the horses around her, but she was totally different when Tally rode her: agreeable, happy, ears perked almost all the time. Some of the school horses at Oaks were reserved for beginners only. Endlessly patient, they'd stand still for as long as needed for beginner riders to mount and get settled in the saddle. The more advanced school horses, like Sweetie, mostly went in jumping lessons and had a variety of riders. Sweetie had very little patience for riders who balanced on her mouth or bounced around too much on her back.

"Guess what?" she whispered to the mare. "We're doing the medal!" Sweetie stuck her muzzle between Tally's arm and her side, looking for a treat.

That's when Tally heard someone round the corner; she hoped it would be one of her friends. It was busy down by Sweetie's stall, with traffic from the boarders' aisle and horses coming in and out from the upper and lower rings. One of the best things about having barn friends, Tally thought, was that it didn't matter if they went to the same school, or even if they were close in age. They had a love of horses in common, and that was enough.

"Hey there," said a male voice she didn't recognize. Tally turned to see a man in a navy blue polo shirt, jeans, and shiny black paddock boots standing in front of Sweetie's stall. "Can you point me toward the office?"

Tally instantly felt her face flush. She hated turning red, but it happened pretty often—usually when she was surprised or embarrassed.

"Up those stairs," Tally said, pointing him toward the other end of the aisle. "The office is right above the tack room for the school horses...it's a separate tack room from the ones the boarders use," she added, immediately feeling foolish for offering this random detail that Polo Guy certainly wouldn't need.

"Thanks," he said, walking down the aisle. "By the way, I'm Ryan."

· CHAPTER 2 ·

"I must have looked like such an idiot, talking to Sweetie like a little kid and then babbling about the separate tack rooms," Tally told her best friend, Kaitlyn Rowe, before their English class started the next day. Kaitlyn, who was twelve and also a seventh grader, took lessons at Oaks as well, so she understood the ins and outs at the barn. It wasn't always easy for Tally to get her friends who didn't ride to understand what went on at Oaks, and why it was all so important to her. If they knew she'd had a show over the weekend, they'd ask her how she did in her "race." It was almost too much work to explain the type of riding she did to someone who didn't understand horses beyond the ones who ran in the Kentucky Derby.

"Don't be so hard on yourself. Everyone talks to

their horses, not just little kids," Kaitlyn said. "And who cares if you told him about the separate tack rooms?"

"Anything you want to share with the rest of us?" Mrs. Bach, the girls' English teacher, instantly silenced every other noise in the classroom as she called them out for chatting. Tally felt her face flush, yet again, and mumbled "sorry" in Mrs. Bach's direction.

The girls waited until their teacher turned on a video—a movie adaptation of the book they'd been reading—to resume their conversation.

"So, who do you think he was?" Kaitlyn asked.

"Maybe a new boarder?" Tally suggested.

"Why would he care where the office was?"

That was a good point. The boarders basically worked through their individual trainers, not the barn manager who oversaw the lesson program at Oaks. But who else could that guy have been? Tally shrugged in response to Kaitlyn and turned her attention to the movie. Anything having to do with horses or riding was far more interesting than English class, but if her grades started to suffer, the first thing her parents would cut would be barn time. It was in her best interest to watch the boring movie.

♘

After English, the rest of the school day moved at a snail's pace until lunchtime, when Tally met Kaitlyn and their friend, Ava Foster, in the cafeteria. Ava was eleven and she rode too, but at a different barn that catered more to ponies. She had an adorable bay with a big white blaze and the cutest show name ever: Stonelea Dance Party. Danny, as he was called at the barn, competed in the Medium Pony Hunters and Ava had another year on him before she'd move up to the large ponies—a transition that didn't seem to faze her in the least. Not much bothered Ava. She just had this way about her, breezing through life. Tally wished she could have an attitude—not to mention a pony—like Ava's.

"Hey guys," Tally said as she approached Kaitlyn and Ava, leaning into the wall at the far end of the cafeteria and sliding her back down it until she was seated. Seventh graders at her school had a tradition of sitting in groups on the floor, rather than at the tables. Tally thought it was a pretty dumb and uncomfortable thing to do, but she wasn't about to call attention to herself by not eating her lunch like everyone else in seventh grade. Besides, there wasn't anyone she'd rather sit with than Kaitlyn and Ava, and they didn't seem to mind.

Just as she sat down, a group of boys from their grade walked past them toward the food line, one of them nodding his head toward Tally. She instinctively followed his gaze and glanced down at her breeches. Tally got picked up right from school for riding on Fridays so she had no choice but to go to school in her riding clothes.

"*Neeeeeeeigh*," the boy whinnied in her direction and the other two laughed. Tally felt her mind race to come up with something to say in response, but Ava beat her to it.

"Wow, never heard that one before. How long did it take you to come up with that?"

Tally was impressed. The boys rolled their eyes and turned their attention to the French fries in the hot food line.

"Like I was saying," Ava said, turning back to Kaitlyn, "I really wanted to try out for the gymnastics team, but there just isn't time with riding." Ava's older sister was an accomplished gymnast and Ava was always talking about how much she wanted to try the sport, too. Tally couldn't imagine wanting to do anything but ride.

"Um, I'll come out and ride Danny for you any time that you have the urge to go flip around some bars," Kaitlyn joked and all three girls laughed.

The last few classes of the day thankfully moved a bit faster. As soon as the bell rang to conclude seventh period, Tally suppressed the urge to canter on foot, and instead sped-walked down the hallway and out to the parking lot where her mom was waiting. Just fifteen minutes later, they pulled into the Oaks parking lot. Tally noticed a pony that she'd never seen before trotting past in the indoor.

"See you at six," her mom said and Tally gave her a wave, already halfway to the entrance of the ring. She glanced at her watch to confirm she had a few minutes before she needed to tack up and slipped into the bleachers on the short end of the ring. Opening her backpack in an attempt to look casual and not like she was ogling this new pony (which she totally was), Tally watched him and his rider trot by again.

They were just warming up, but the rider had a look in her eye like she was staring down a massive triple combination. It was a steely expression, deter-mined, like she was really thinking about what was going on underneath her. The pony practically floated across the arena, his huge stride accentuated by its front white socks that came up almost all the way to his knees. Like Sweetie, this pony was a chestnut, but his coat gleamed in a way that Tally had never seen before in person. Feeling herself staring, she rum-maged through her bag again, aware that she proba-bly wasn't doing such a good job of being casual. Tally pulled her red, weathered Quince Oaks baseball cap out of her bag and threaded her wavy brown ponytail through it, pulling the brim down over her eyes. The pony passed the bleachers again, and Tally checked out his rider this time.

"Good boy," she heard the rider say softly as she slowed the pony's trot down and sank into the saddle to sit the trot. Tally noticed the telltale silver diamond on the rider's tall boots, signaling a high-end brand that she noticed in lots of horse show photographs. The rider's blonde hair was neatly contained inside a hair-net under her helmet, and her polo shirt was tucked into her tan breeches, accented by a wide belt, with the buckle placed on the side over the zipper on her hip.

Why get so dressed up just to trot around? Tally wondered. This afternoon, she was dressed pretty typically for her own lessons—tee shirt, breeches in a fun color (today they were light blue) and half chaps with paddock boots. She'd go back to breaking in her new tall boots another day. Watching this girl trot around was almost like seeing some sort of exotic animal. If she looked this put together at Oaks, what must she look like at shows?

Tally glanced at her watch again and got up to go check her horse assignment in the office. She was usually riding Sweetie, but with such a busy lesson program, riders didn't always get their first pick. So the office was the first stop to confirm each lesson's mount. Tally eased herself down off the bleachers and began walking toward the tack room. As the pony walked past her, his rider looked at her and smiled.

"Hey," Tally said.

"Hi," the girl replied, her smile warm and genuine.

"How's he doing?" a loud voice called out.

"Fine," Tally heard the rider reply as she rounded the corner by the school tack room. An older bay pony named Little Bit (Lil for her barn name) was housed in the stall right next to the stairs that went up to the office. Tally fished out a treat from her bag and fed it to Lil before jogging up the old wooden staircase, which creaked under her. Finding out her horse for the day always provided a little rush of excitement.

Tally walked through the door at the top of the stairs but paused before getting to the barn secretary who had the day's lesson assignments. Looking down at the ring from the office's floor-to-ceiling windows, she took in a sharp breath. Teaching the girl on the pony with the floaty trot was none other than Polo Guy himself.

CHAPTER 3

Tally couldn't make out what Polo Guy was saying from up in the office with the windows closed, but she watched as he made some hand gestures to the rider, who promptly guided her pony to the rail and picked up a canter, smooth as glass. That was the best feeling, Tally thought to herself, when a horse just lifts into the canter from the walk, without those hurried trot steps in between.

"Earth to Tally...you're riding Sweetie today. And in about ten minutes, I might add, so you probably want to think about getting a move on. Lesson is up in the outdoor today."

Tally blushed and thanked Marsha, the barn secretary, before jogging down the steps to get ready for her lesson. She didn't realize how much time she'd spent ogling that pony. And Polo Guy was his trainer!

Down in the tack room, she gathered up her helmet, Sweetie's saddle, pads, and bridle and then hurried down the aisle, hoping that the mare hadn't rolled in the mud overnight.

"Hi, pony," she said affectionately when she reached Sweetie's stall. At 14.3 or 15 hands (depending on who you asked), Sweetie was, quite frankly, an undesirable height for showing. She was just a couple inches too big to compete in the large pony division, and her size would keep her from being competitive over big fences in the horse divisions. At shows, horses and ponies had to make it down the lines—two jumps in a row with a set number of strides between them. The smaller your horse's stride, the more difficult it would be to make the numbers. This wasn't such a problem at the barn's in-house schooling shows, where the lines were set shorter with a school horse's step in mind, but it would be a stretch for Sweetie to do the numbers at a bigger show.

Tally groomed Sweetie quickly with a hard brush and the mare pinned her ears to express her distaste for the rushed treatment. Sweetie usually preferred a more relaxing grooming.

"Sorry, girl," Tally whispered, "We're in a hurry today." She tacked Sweetie up fast, something else the little school horse wasn't thrilled about, and walked her out of the stall and out the aisle, glancing again at her watch as they walked. She had two minutes before the lesson started. "New record," Tally whispered under her breath.

Up at the ring, a couple of riders were flatting their horses. The two girls with whom Tally usually took lessons, Maggie and Jordan, were walking around the ring with each of their horses on a loose rein. Tally mounted quickly and Sweetie tossed her head and walked toward the rail just as Tally put her right foot in the stirrup. The mare did not like being hurried.

"Hey guys," Meg said as she strode into the ring. "Let's make sure we walk a full lap and then pick up a posting trot."

The girls settled into the usual rhythm of the flatwork at the start of all their lessons, and Meg threw in some more unusual exercises—aimed at getting ready for the medal class, Tally thought with a little thrill.

"Drop your irons," Meg called. Tally kept her calves as firm as she could against Sweetie's sides as she slipped her feet out of her stirrups. As soon as Sweetie felt the irons moving against her barrel she scooted forward a little bit, and Tally sank deeper into the saddle, whispering "whoa" to the mare.

"Good, Tal," Meg said, "Just keep riding through that. She'll settle. Maggie, did I say to stop trotting?"

Tally stifled a smile. She'd learned by riding with Meg not to change her horse's gait at a show (or in lessons, for that matter) unless the judge or instructor specifically asked for it. She thought about the rider on the shiny chestnut pony down in the smaller indoor. She had a great position—that was obvious from just the couple of minutes that Tally watched her. Tally stretched up a bit taller in the saddle as she continued sitting the trot without her stirrups.

"I saw that, Tally. Nice work sitting up tall, hold that there."

The lesson continued with the girls recovering their stirrups, then jumping a gymnastic, followed by a small course of jumps. When it was time to walk their horses and cool out, Meg suggested that Tally, Maggie, and Jordan take a walk around the property, a little treat reserved for the most competent riders in the lesson program. Maggie, a Black rider the same age as Tally, walked up next to her once they were past the gate of the outdoor ring. Both girls were about 5'3", so they ended up riding a lot of the same horses in the Oaks lesson program. Tally had watched plenty of lessons where Maggie rode Sweetie, and vice versa.

"Sweetie looked really good today. She's jumping *so* cute," Maggie said.

Tally thanked her friend, enjoying the familiar thrill that followed a great lesson.

After a meandering stroll around the property aboard their horses, the girls dismounted at the entrance to the school aisle. Tally led Sweetie to her stall where she untacked the mare, who began happily munching on some hay in the corner the moment the bit was out of her mouth. Tally then walked the saddle, pads and bridle back to the tack room before slipping on Sweetie's halter to hand graze her outside. There was still a good twenty minutes before her mom would pick her up, but Tally never minded the extra time hanging out at the barn.

The large, triangular patch of grass between the paths to the big rings and the trails apparently had the best grazing on the property because Sweetie practically dragged Tally over to it.

"You don't want to go up to the top of the hill?" Tally asked with a laugh. That was their usual spot, but the mare seemed to have made up her mind.

Tally let the lead rope go slack as she watched Sweetie graze. It was always so peaceful, just the two of them.

"Hey!" chirped someone behind her, yanking Tally out of her solitude.

"Oh, hi," she said instinctively before it even registered who'd come up next to them. It was the new girl and her cute chestnut.

"I'm Mac," the girl said. "Well, Mackenzie, actually, but everyone calls me Mac."

Huh. Going by a nickname was Tally's thing. What were the odds that this new girl would do the same?

"Nice to meet you, I'm Tally."

"Telly?"

"No, *Tally*. It's actually short for Natalia."

"You go by your nickname, too!" Mac said with an easy, broad smile, further annoying Tally with her sincere delight over their commonality. "What's your pony's name?"

"Sweetie. And she's actually just tall enough to be a horse but she gets mistaken for a pony a lot. How about yours?" asked Tally, gesturing to Mac's pony, who was somehow even more adorable up close.

"Joey," Mac said, and the pony flicked an ear in her direction from his grazing spot near Sweetie who, inexplicably, was happy to share her space with this new Oaks resident. *Traitor*, thought Tally, smiling to herself. She knew she wasn't giving Mac a fair chance, but here was this girl who went by a nickname that was cooler than hers, and with a dream pony of her very own. Tally was jealous, plain and simple.

"He kept checking himself out in those mirrors in the indoor," Mac said with a laugh.

"Yeah, it takes new horses and ponies a while to adjust to that ring. There are a lot of mirrors." Tally couldn't help it. This girl was so genuinely nice and easy to talk to that she felt her jealousy melting away.

"Ryan says we'll lesson in one of those big rings up top this week," Mac continued. "The jumps in that ring are so pretty."

"Thanks, we actually just had a jump-painting party a couple weeks ago."

"Oh, that sounds like fun. My old barn was really small and there weren't other kids or even other pony riders."

Mac went on to explain to Tally that she used to board Joey at a private barn about twenty minutes away from Oaks. She'd worked with a couple of different trainers before finding Ryan.

"He is just the best," she said. "Really tough, but not mean like some of the other people I rode with." Mac looked down to her pocket and pulled out her phone. Glancing at a text, she clucked at Joey and looked up to Tally.

"That's my ride. It was nice meeting you."

"Nice meeting you too," Tally said, really meaning it now that she had gotten over the nickname thing. "I'll see you around."

· CHAPTER 4 ·

"Hey Tal, did you get my note?"

So it *was* her dad. Tally and her parents (she was an only child) were having dinner together that night after Tally's lesson.

"Yeah, but I'm not really sure I get it."

"What's not to get?"

Tally stopped herself just as she was about to roll her eyes. Her parents, James and Stacy Hart, hated when she did that. "I don't know, it was about talent and hard work and how...both are important?"

Her dad set his fork down and wiped his hands on the napkin in his lap—always a stickler for manners.

"Hard work beats talent when talent doesn't work hard," he repeated from the note in her grooming box. "You're winning all these ribbons, which you know I think is great. You're very talented and I'm proud of you. But I left that little reminder with your riding stuff because I want you to remember that riding, or any sport, is about more than just having that raw, natural talent. You have to put the work in, too."

What began as a feeling of happiness from her dad's praise had fizzled into frustration and Tally opened her mouth to respond. But her father held his hand up and continued: "If you want to move up the ranks, you have to match, or even exceed, your talent with hard work. Really hard work. Because there are other kids who want this as much as you do and they're putting in the time."

"Dad, I ride twice a week and work hard at the barn to pay for that second lesson. Don't you think—" Tally began, suddenly feeling super defensive.

"I know, and I think that's awesome," her father quickly added. "I just think it can't hurt to remind you that it's sometimes the hardest worker in the room—and not necessarily the most talented one— who's gonna get that blue ribbon. It's really good that you do so well in your lessons and at shows, but maybe that's a sign that it's time to push yourself harder to get to that next level, don't you think?"

Once the family had finished eating, Tally was angrily loading up their dinner plates into the dishwasher. Why was her father on this work harder kick anyway? Wasn't it a good sign that she always got compliments in her lessons and did well in the horse shows?

The next afternoon, Tally was dropping off her show registration and check at the barn while her mother waited in the car. "Fifteen minutes," her mom said sternly, knowing how easily Tally could lose track of time at Oaks. Tally walked briskly toward the tack room and headed straight for her grooming box without bothering to turn on the light. As her eyes adjusted to the dim, dusty light, she fished through spare gloves and old hairnets in the box for the note.

HARD WORK BEATS TALENT WHEN TALENT DOESN'T WORK HARD.

She read it back to herself slowly. *So, basically, a really hard worker can beat someone who is talented when the talented person doesn't work hard enough. Yeah, well, what else is new?* She folded the note back up, stuck it under a brush, and left the tack room for the office.

"Get the canter you need before you're on your way to the jump, Mac. Come on, how many times do I have to say the same thing?"

Tally froze right outside the tack room at the sound of Ryan's voice carrying through the arena. She walked toward the end of the aisle, stopping before she hit the corner.

The ring had gone quiet except for the sound of Joey cantering. *One two three, one two three, one two three*, Tally counted along automatically as she heard the pony go by.

"Sit straight, sit straight, why are you leaning? Stop a minute," Ryan bellowed.

After a moment of quiet, she heard Ryan ask Mac something, and then Mac softly replied: "I'm looking for the distance."

"There are no distances. Only rhythm," Ryan told her. "If your pony is straight and you've got a steady canter rhythm, the distances will come up. It won't always be the exact same distance, but a reasonable one will be there if you've got the straightness and the rhythm. You're so focused on that takeoff spot that you're ignoring what you need to be doing before you get to the jump. And you still don't have that pace that you need! Ring speed. Do it again."

Tally peeked around the corner just in time to see her new friend and her pony pop up over a single oxer.

"Better. You can quit with that, but drop your stirrups and post for four laps before you let him walk."

Whoa. This guy is no joke, Tally thought, secretly happy that Meg was never that tough on her. Wait... was this the kind of hard work her dad was talking about that he thought she wasn't doing? Lost in thought, Tally didn't notice Ryan turn the corner until they were practically face-to-face.

"Oh, hey. Tally, right?" Ryan said to her, friendly and breezy, like he hadn't just been screaming his head off at Mac.

"Hey," Tally replied, trying not to let her face go red this time. Ryan continued walking past her to the parking lot and Tally hurried around to the stairs, taking them two at a time up to the office to drop off her paperwork. Ryan made her a little nervous, and she was hoping that exchange was it for the day. Still, she was intrigued by his teaching style and the general air he had about him. He seemed like a really big deal and she was eager to learn why.

Up in the office, Tally brought her paperwork to Marsha. She was on the phone so she smiled and nodded at Tally in response as she collected the papers. Tally walked slowly back to the stairs, keeping an eye on the indoor ring below. Mac had that steely look on her face again as she trotted down the long side. Her leg was so solid against her pony as she posted, high but soft, that Tally almost forgot that she didn't have her stirrups.

Downstairs, Tally chatted with a girl from her school who'd started taking lessons at Oaks and said a quick hello to Meg as she speed-walked down the aisle. Her instructor looked distracted and maybe a little sad, Tally thought to herself. With a little more time before she needed to meet her mom at the car, Tally decided to walk the long way around the barn, maybe catch Mac and give Joey a treat before she headed home. Giving quick pats to some of her favorite horses as she walked down the school aisle, Tally stopped, of course, at Sweetie's stall for a moment with her favorite mare. Then, rounding the top end of the barn and heading to the boarders' aisle, she noticed that Joey's stall was in the same position as Sweetie's, at the far end of his aisle, just on the other side of the barn. Mac was putting her saddle on a rack outside the stall while Joey stood quietly on the cross ties. Tally noticed his show name on the plate affixed to his stall: Smoke Hill Jet Set.

"Hey Mac," she said, just as her new friend turned around. Her face was red and she'd obviously been crying. "What's wrong?"

Mac wiped under her eyes with the back of her black riding gloves. "Oh, you know, the usual. I chipped, like, every jump in my lesson and Ryan hates me," Mac said between sniffles.

"He sounds tough," Tally replied honestly.

"Yeah, but he's right. I don't have an eye. People can just canter right out of the turn and sit there and the distance just comes up for them. How does that happen?" Perfect, put-together Mac was talking fast and crying hard now.

"Your leg is amazing though," Tally offered, fumbling for the words to make her friend feel better while remembering Mac's impressive posting trot without stirrups.

"Huh?" Mac replied, looking confused.

"Oh, I, um, saw you posting without your stirrups while I was up in the office. I almost didn't realize you didn't have them because you were just posting like normal. I could never do that."

"Thanks," Mac replied, taking a deep, shuddering breath. "But that's just because Ryan's always making me do laps without stirrups."

"It was probably just a bad lesson," Tally offered, hoping to keep Mac from crying again. "I'm sure it will get better." Mac sniffed again and hung up the bridle she'd been holding, then went over to give Joey a scratch on his mane.

"Thanks," Mac said. "I hope so. My old pony and I were doing so well together in the children's ponies. We were champion or reserve at most shows. I knew that moving up to the division would be harder, but I didn't know it would be *this* hard. Maybe I was only good enough to do the children's, you know? We've been to like, five shows already in the division and it's just not working out."

Realizing she was probably overdue to meet her mom, Tally reached into her pocket for Joey's treat.

"You're way more experienced than me, but I'm sure it's just a matter of time before you're winning again. Hey, I'm sorry, but I've got to run. Can he have a peppermint?"

"Sure. It's not his fault I suck."

"Stop it, you do not!" Tally said, ducking underneath the cross tie and letting Joey lip the peppermint off her palm. "I have to run or my mom's going to kill me, but I'll see you soon, okay?"

"See ya," Mac said, taking a currycomb to Joey's shoulder.

Walking down the aisle to the parking lot, Tally felt unsettled. How could someone like Mac—with the fancy pony and the big shows, plus that rock-solid leg—think that she was bad at riding?

· CHAPTER 5 ·

"Good job, ladies, now walk and come on into the middle, please."

Tally gave Scout, a bay gelding and her mount for the week's Wednesday lesson, a pat on his neck. He pulled down on the reins in response to stretch out his long neck. Scout was taller at 16 hands, and a different ride than Sweetie. They'd worked on collecting and extending the canter in this particular lesson, jumping a line of small verticals first in six strides, then extending for five strides, then collecting for six again. At first, the exercise wasn't easy for Tally and the best she seemed to be able to manage was five strides and then kind of a half stride or stutter step instead of the quiet six strides. She looked forward to trying it again in their next lesson on Friday.

The riders congregated in the middle of the ring

while one of the boarders took her horse out to the rail, collecting him into a rounded canter.

"I have some news," Meg began, and Tally felt her breath catch in her throat. Having news usually didn't mean good news, she'd learned.

"I was offered a job coaching the equestrian team at the college where I went down in Florida," Meg began. Tally thought her instructor might start to cry. "It was a very hard decision to make because I love teaching you all, but it's the right move for my career...so this will be our last lesson together."

Jordan and Maggie looked shell-shocked and Tally felt her eyes fill with tears, which stung as they rolled down her sweaty cheeks. Tally had learned almost everything she knew about horses and riding from Meg. Her instructor looked down, brushing her hands on her jeans.

"I know it's hard, but change is good. Really. You'll learn so much more having a new instructor, too. It's always good to ride with more than one person. It's been a pleasure teaching you girls and I know you'll continue to learn and do well."

"So, who will be teaching us now?" Maggie asked.

Tally was so upset by Meg's news that she didn't even consider who would teach their lessons going forward.

"Well, that's the good news," Meg said, her mood visibly brightening. Have you met the new hunter jumper trainer, Ryan? He came here with a bunch of his clients who moved their horses to Oaks from their old barns. Go to the boarders' aisle and say hi. He and his clients regularly show on the A Circuit. I think you'll learn a lot from him."

Back in the school tack room after putting their horses away, the girls were still reeling from the news.

"I've heard he's tough," said Jordan.

"He is," Tally replied automatically as she dug through her grooming box for a treat for Scout.

The other girls looked at Tally quizzically.

"Oh, I've seen him teach that new girl, Mac, a couple of times," Tally explained to Maggie and Jordan. "His lessons look a lot harder than Meg's." Then she remembered when she first met Ryan and he was looking for the office. He was probably going to talk to Marsha or the barn manager, Brenna, because he knew he'd be taking on this new job.

All three girls were quiet as they finished up in the

tack room. Tally let herself into Scout's stall to feed
him a carrot while her mind raced. Could she ride
with someone like Ryan? The way she saw him being
so hard on Mac, she wasn't sure she was tough enough
for that kind of training.

"Just in case I don't see you before I fly out..." Tally
turned to see Meg standing outside of Scout's stall
with her arms outstretched. Tally ducked under the
stall guard and hugged Meg hard, feeling the hot tears
sting in her eyes again.

"You're a naturally talented rider," Meg whispered
to her. "And I know you love the horses. You could
go far with this. It's scary when you start to ride with
someone new, but you're lucky that it's Ryan. He's
the real deal and he's going to teach you a lot. Stay in
touch, okay? I'll miss you, kiddo."

Tally felt choked up, unsure of what to say to
her longtime instructor and how to package all her
feelings into some sort of meaningful goodbye. She
couldn't think of a way to do it well, so she settled for
simplicity instead.

"Thanks," Tally said softly. "I'll really miss you."

Meg gave her another quick squeeze and then

turned on her heel, striding down the aisle toward the parking lot.

As she took a shaky breath, Tally watched Meg walk away. "Change is good," she could imagine her dad saying. But what could possibly be good about losing the person who had taught her so much about horses and riding?

CHAPTER 6

"So that's it. Meg's leaving—she just told us out of nowhere, and now we have to ride with Ryan, who totally scares me," Tally told her friends in gym class the next day. They had just run The Mile, an unfortunate event that came up a couple times a year, and their gym teacher had instructed the class to walk an extra lap around the track to cool down. Just like they did with the horses, Tally thought to herself with a little smile.

"Ryan McNeil?" Ava asked her. "I see him at shows a lot. Everybody loves him."

"They do?" Tally asked, incredulous.

"He's tough but he's fair," Ava continued. "You should see some of these other trainers. They're either too nice and their riders don't improve, or they're mean and make the riders feel bad. Ryan wants to help you ride better and he does. I was in the same section of smalls as one of his kids at Pony Finals."

"What's Pony Finals?" Kaitlyn asked. Tally was glad she spoke up—she hadn't heard of it either but it sounded important.

"They have it in Kentucky every year in August, and you qualify for it if you're champion or reserve at an A show. It's one of the biggest shows of the year and basically like this huge pony party with no horses and, like, a thousand kids. There's so much to do when you're not riding, and then for the show you have just the model and hack and one jumping class. That's it. It's a lot of pressure with only one trip and there are hundreds of ponies so most people don't even get a ribbon but it's great experience."

There was so much that Ava just said that Tally didn't understand, but the girls rounded the last bend of the track and there wouldn't be time to figure it all out.

"Did *you* get a ribbon at Pony Finals?" Kaitlyn asked, her eyes wide. Tally wondered the same thing. A hundred ponies in a division? When classes at the

Oaks schooling shows had more horses than ribbons, Tally considered them big. The idea that she might not get a ribbon at all raised the stakes and made her heart race. In a good way.

"No, but we were twenty-sixth overall out of, like, one hundred and ten, so we were happy," Ava said with a shrug.

The shrill sound of the gym teacher's whistle halted the girls' conversation.

"Okay class, let's get changed and move on to sixth period!"

That night before dinner, Tally's mom asked her to come into the kitchen. Marsha from the barn had called to say that Ryan would pick up Meg's lesson schedule starting the following week, so Tally's work shift would be moved to Friday. Which meant she wouldn't get to ride.

"But the show is on Sunday," Tally realized out loud, feeling that same lump in her throat that came with Meg's news. "Can I still do it? Will Ryan coach us?"

Her mother, stirring a pot on the stove with one hand and setting a timer with the other, didn't seem to pick up on the mild panic in her daughter's voice.

"I don't know, honey, she didn't say. Ask Marsha tomorrow."

The rest of the night, Tally felt restless. Too many things were changing. She looked at the photo she'd framed of herself and Meg and Sweetie with a blue ribbon from a schooling show at Oaks. The frame, which she'd made out of popsicle sticks at horse camp last summer, looked like a little kid had slapped it together. Suddenly feeling disgusted with the childish project, she carefully removed the photo and tossed the frame in her trash can. She tucked the picture in between her bedside lamp and alarm clock and settled into bed with a book, hoping to distract herself from the memory of hugging Meg goodbye.

The next morning, Tally woke up to her alarm clock's jarring melody and hit the snooze button, opening one eye to glance at the time. *7:30? Was she late for school?* Bleary-eyed, Tally remembered that it was an in-service day at her middle school and she'd be doing her shift at the barn that morning. She got dressed, grabbed a bottle of water and a pack of Pop-Tarts from the kitchen, and met her mom in the driveway. She planned to drop Tally off at Oaks before she went to work.

As soon as she arrived at the barn, Tally went to the boarders' aisle to look for Mac. A couple horses stood on cross ties getting groomed while a rider stood outside the tack room cleaning her saddle. The aisle smelled of horses, fly spray, and leather conditioner. Tally never understood why her parents joked about their cars stinking like a barn. To her, the smells were wonderful.

"Hey!" Mac emerged from the boarders' tack room, adjusting her hair into a hairnet. "I was hoping to see you here. I heard you're going to ride with Ryan now, that's so exciting."

"Yeah, well, I don't know," Tally replied. "I'm really nervous about it. I've rarely ridden with anyone but Meg."

"Seriously?" Mac asked, looking truly baffled.

"Yeah. He seems really hard."

"He is," Mac began, snapping the harness on her helmet before turning her attention to Joey's saddle pads. "But he really knows what he's doing. Moving up to the division has been so hard but the way he breaks things down in my lessons, I'm actually excited to go to the next show."

How could anyone not be excited to show? Tally wondered. But before she tackled that question, she was ready to get to the bottom of all this new terminology she talked about with Ava earlier in the week.

"Okay, wait, so what is 'the division,' and what are 'the hack' and 'the model?'"

"Whoa, one thing at a time. Is this a test?" Mac asked with a laugh.

"No, no," Tally said, smiling. "My friend Ava was talking about it at school yesterday, but I didn't get a chance to ask her before our class ended. She went to Pony Finals last year—she rides a pony named Danny."

"Ava Foster?"

"Yeah."

"She is *such* a good rider." Mac was wide-eyed now, a look of reverence on her face. "I watched another girl from her barn schooling Danny once when he was stopping. That pony is not an easy ride."

This was news to Tally, who had always kind of assumed when ponies were that nice and that fancy, they had to be more of a push-button, automatic ride.

"Anyway, the hack is your flat class in a hunter division. They call it the under saddle. The model is when the judge looks at your pony's conformation—the way its body is put together. And the division is the regular pony hunters. It's a big step up from Short Stirrup or the Children's Pony Hunters. The lines are set longer, the jumps are bigger and you can't make the mistakes that you can get away with in the children's ponies. You really have to nail it. Like, be perfect every trip to get a good ribbon. There's no conformation or jog in the children's either, just in the division. You can ride smalls until you're twelve, mediums until you're fourteen, and any junior can show a large."

Mac had finished tacking up Joey as she spoke and now had her arm slung over the pony's neck. His eyes were halfway closed—he looked perfectly happy to stand by, motionless while his rider chatted.

"So Joey could make mistakes in the children's ponies too?" Tally asked.

"Oh no, I had another pony for the children's. We bought Joey to do the division. I've only been riding him for a few months."

Tally couldn't even imagine owning *one* fancy pony, let alone one for each division.

"Ryan has us jump higher in lessons than we do at the shows so the jumps don't look so big there," Mac continued. Tally was glad to see that her friend was in a happier mood about her riding today. "It's fun, but it can be a little scary."

"How high are you jumping?"

"In lessons, 2'9", sometimes even three-foot out of the lines to get us used to it so the jumps look smaller at shows."

"What? How big are the jumps in the horse show?"

"For the mediums, they're 2'6". But it's a big 2'6". I'm thirteen, but I show as twelve because my birthday is in March. So I have a couple more years of showing mediums in the division."

Tally was stunned at how much she'd learned in this short talk with Mac. The jumps in her hunter division at Oaks were also 2'6", but Meg was always saying that the schooling show lines were set short, and the jumps were a 'soft' 2'6". She didn't think she'd ever jumped 3' in a lesson before. The school horses worked hard in their lessons all week so the instructors were careful not to over jump them.

"I'm going to hack Joey in the outdoor ring. Want to come?"

Tally was so lost in thought that she took an awkwardly long time to answer Mac's question.

"Oh, I wish I could, but I'm actually working today. I usually lesson on Fridays but Meg already left for Florida and Ryan isn't teaching my lesson until next week."

The girls said goodbye and Tally set off for work. Over the next two hours, Tally filled dozens of water buckets—soaking her sneakers and jean shorts in the process—and distributed a flake of hay to every horse on the school side of the barn. With just enough time to clean her tack for the show before her mom came to pick her up, Tally settled into the school tack room to condition Sweetie's saddle. She read a lot of horse show blogs and magazines and loved the idea of perfecting everything she could for showing—even if it was just a schooling show. She loved paying attention to all the little details.

She had no idea how many new details she was about to discover.

· CHAPTER 7 ·

"Walk, please. All walk...And canter, please. All canter."

When Tally reached the top of the hill, her heart started beating faster. She loved the sound of the announcer's voice coming over the PA system. And while jumping classes at a show were obviously more exciting, there was something about the commands of a flat class that got her adrenaline going. Picking up each gait quickly and crisply while maintaining her position was such a good feeling.

It was still early enough in the show day that she didn't feel hot in her show clothes—the tan Euroseat breeches that she saved for shows, a white show shirt with a purple floral lining inside the collar and cuffs, and her softshell navy hunt coat.

She felt like a million bucks in her show clothes,

especially when she had on her lucky socks (royal blue with cream and green horseshoes) underneath her still-uncomfortable tall boots. She couldn't find that pair of socks this morning but she wasn't too concerned. Sweetie had been so good in her lessons—she probably wouldn't need the luck of a special pair of socks to do well in this show.

Tally checked in at the viewing area of the indoor ring, which doubled as the show office on schooling show days. Marsha handed her the day's number, 110, and Tally tied it around her waist.

"You've probably got about twelve trips to go in this division and the next before your medal class will start," Marsha told her.

"Thanks, Marsha," Tally said and headed back down for the barn.

"Hey, Tally, did you learn your course?"

Ryan. Tally mentally willed herself to keep from blushing.

"Not yet. I was going to tack up Sweetie first."

"Well come on, then," he said with a smile as he gestured toward the course diagrams posted by the gate. "I'll go over your course with you."

Tally had assumed she'd take some lessons with Ryan before showing with him, but apparently this would be Day One with her new trainer. Suddenly the horse show butterflies in her stomach were joined by new trainer butterflies.

"Okay, so you're starting out with that red vertical on the diagonal there, coming toward home," Ryan began. "So I'd walk in the ring, pick up your right lead by the time you get to the outside line, and go straight to your first jump."

"So, no courtesy circle?" Tally asked.

Ryan paused, with something of a quizzical look on his face before answering. "This is your medal class, right? And the first jump is all the way at the other end of the ring from the in gate. No circle—you want to get right to it and get to your first jump, and then minimize the distance between your fences. Kind of like a handy class. Make sense?"

I guess this is my first lesson with Ryan after all, Tally thought to herself. She nodded yes.

"Okay, so after that you're going to roll back to the vertical in your outside line. When you land off that first jump, be sure to really put your left leg on so she knows where she's going and doesn't think she's doing the whole diagonal line. Hold your left rein and bend her around to jump two on the outside. Then you'll turn right and catch that skinny style jump at the far end of the ring. Keep her straight so you make sure she sees it. Then you'll jump the whole judge's line in five strides. Bring her down to a trot and come up the quarter line for your trot fence here. I'd get your trot before the corner, otherwise she might think you're pulling her up before the jump. You'll land cantering and come around and catch your diagonal line in six strides. If you want to be really slick, see if you can get her down to a trot in the corner and then walk before you go out of the ring. But if you've got a lot of horse and you need to circle at the end, that's fine too."

Tally felt like her head was going to spin right off her body. She'd learned a lot in Meg's lessons but never this much information, this fast.

"Feel like you've got it?" Ryan asked. Tally thought he might be smirking at her.

"I think so. It's a lot to remember. I'll have to go over it a few more times in my head, I think," Tally said, glancing from the course diagram to the ring and back again.

"See? Better to learn your course before you tack up," Ryan said with a wink. "You don't want to feel rushed learning the course. I'll see you back up here soon."

Tally repeated the jumps in order to herself as she walked down to the barn, let herself into Sweetie's stall where she went over the mare's coat with a soft brush before tacking up.

"Vertical, rollback to the corner, skinny jump, outside line, trot fence, diagonal line," she whispered, gathering her reins to walk Sweetie up the hill.

Repeating the course for a final time, Tally realized she'd forgotten some of Ryan's more specific instructions. When was she supposed to bring Sweetie down to the trot for the trot jump? And how many strides was the diagonal line?

"Two trips away until the junior medal," the announcer said over the PA. Tally hurried to mount up, unsure of where she would go in the order.

"I put you in fifth, so we've got time to flat and do a couple jumps in the schooling ring," Ryan said, suddenly right in front of Tally and Sweetie. It was

☙

like the guy could read her mind…and be in three places at once. "Ready?"

Tally nodded and, with her heels, nudged Sweetie toward the schooling ring.

"Go ahead and do a lap or two at the trot to the left, then canter a lap. Then do it the other way," Ryan called to her as he swiftly removed the pin from a jump cup and adjusted it to make a low oxer.

Tally followed his instructions and focused on pushing her heels down and opening up her shoulders.

"Your lower leg is way out in front of you. Work on pulling it further back, behind the girth, and sit softly in the middle of the saddle for your post. Stay out of the back seat."

Huh. She'd never heard that about her position from Meg before.

Pulling her lower leg back felt slightly unnatural but Tally wanted to do as she was told.

"Now change directions, trot a little to the right and then canter a lap…lower leg back a little bit more… there. Perfect. Keep it right where it is. We'll work on your position more in lessons."

Tally thought back to her conversation with Mac

about Ryan and she could already see how he could make her a better rider. As long as she could remember everything he said. But she'd think about getting to know Ryan later. For now, it was almost her turn in the medal and she was excited to show him what she could do.

"Walk a lap and then let's catch this little vertical here a couple times."

Sweetie let out a big sigh as Tally let her walk on a looser rein. The other horses whizzing by in the schooling ring—with more cantering past them in the indoor—added to Tally's excitement. She couldn't wait to get in the ring.

After warming up over a vertical a couple of times, then an oxer in the other direction, Ryan deemed her ready to go in. Tally smiled. It was the best feeling when she first stepped into the show ring. It always felt like the butterflies in her stomach all stopped flapping their wings at once, as if her nervousness literally melted away. And she put on her game face.

"Next to show in the Quince Oaks Junior Equitation Medal is number 110, Tally Hart, riding Sweet Talker."

Tally walked into the ring a few strides and then

remembered what Ryan told her: right lead canter, go directly to the first jump. As they approached the outside line, Tally signaled the mare with her left leg and off they went, into a nice medium canter. Maybe she'd even *win* the medal her first time in the class, Tally thought with a flutter of excitement. She turned the corner to the first jump, the vertical with the red rails going toward home. She measured the distance, which came up just right. The mare landed off the vertical and Tally exhaled. It was always a relief to get over the first jump.

Sweetie kept cantering and Tally's mind went blank. What was jump two? Was it the second jump of the line? No! It was the rollback! Forgetting all about Ryan's instructions to use her outside aids to shape the turn, Tally picked up her inside rein and spun Sweetie abruptly to the right to make the rollback. The little mare pinned her ears at Tally's harsh command. Unbalanced, and therefore unable to change her lead, Sweetie held the counter canter in an awkward rollback turn to jump two.

Tally gritted her teeth and put her leg on the little Thoroughbred to make sure they made it over. The mare had jumped the fence crooked so they weren't set up for the turn to jump three, the style fence. But Tally pressed on, opening her inside rein to guide Sweetie to the skinny jump. Never one to refuse if she could help it, Sweetie tried her best to clear the rails between the narrow-set standards, but she never got straight and knocked the top rail out of the cups with her front feet.

It only got worse from there. Sweetie stumbled as she tried to clear the rail she'd knocked over, which set them up for a chip at the in of the judge's line. They got out of the line in six strides, maybe even six and a half. Tally was so frazzled, she wasn't sure. And they blew past the corner before Tally remembered to slow her horse down to a trot, so they didn't get the transition until right before the trot fence, which Sweetie awkwardly popped over. With just the diagonal line to go, and tears threatening to spill down Tally's face before she and Sweetie were even out of the ring, she guided the mare down to jump the first fence again. Not accounting for the horse's shorter stride (and what ended up being a quiet jump into the line), they had another spectacular chip at the oxer on the way out.

Way to finish, Tally thought bitterly. Cantering past the gate, having forgotten about the plan to be slick and walk out without circling, Tally saw Ryan rub his hands down his face and turn away.

Her closing circle was supposed to be a time for feeling elated and accomplished, for completing a course in the show ring that was better than the one before. But this closing circle featured a brand new thought for Tally: She couldn't wait for the show day to be over.

CHAPTER 8

The rest of the show was a blur for Tally. She'd finished a disappointing (but not at all surprising) eighth in the medal out of ten or so riders. She kicked herself for daydreaming about winning when, in the end, she barely got around. For the first time at a show, Tally didn't even feel happy to be there. It was embarrassing to mess up so badly in the medal.

"It's okay," Ryan had told her when he finally resurfaced several medal trips after her own. But his tone didn't sound like it was okay at all. When would they do the recap of the awful course? Or would she have a clean slate when they started lessons? Slightly distracted, Tally and Sweetie jumped around the predictable outside-diagonal-outside-diagonal courses in their low hunter division. Tally missed a lead change here and a distance there but nothing really seemed to register. The whole day just felt like a huge bummer. She gathered up her fourth and fifth place ribbons from the low hunters (last time they'd been reserve champion, she thought, dejectedly) and met her dad down by the tack room to drive home.

"Don't forget to label those," her dad said, nodding at the white and pink rosettes. Tally had actually been considering just throwing them out.

"Why? This isn't exactly a show I want to remember."

"I've told you this before, Tal. Sometimes you win, sometimes you learn. And you know I think you should label the back of every ribbon. You'll look back at them one day and be happy you did."

Back home, Tally put her riding stuff away, showered, and sat down on her bed where she'd tossed the day's ribbons. Her dad was right; it was fun to read what she'd written on the back of old ribbons. If it was a blue, red, or yellow ribbon—or, even better, a tricolor—it was always nice to read the notes on the back and relive the great show days. And if it wasn't a great class, she'd make a note about something that she'd learned or what went on during the day. It was satisfying to look back on that and see how far she'd come. One day, she hoped, she'd look back on this icky show day and think, *wow, I ride so much better than that now.*

On the back of her 4th place ribbon, Tally scribbled, "Sweetie, Oaks schooling show, Low Hunter. 8 horses, OK trip. No ribbon in medal bc it SUCKED." And on the 5th place, "Sweetie, Oaks schooling show, Low Hunter. 8 horses, meh trip."

That afternoon, Kaitlyn invited her to the mall and Tally did her best to put the show out of her mind while they looked for earrings and belts at the accessory store. After shopping, they bought soft pretzels and lemonades and sat in the food court. When Kaitlyn asked about the show, Tally felt like she might start crying to her friend.

"It was just so bad. Maybe the worst trip I've ever had, in a show or even a lesson," Tally said.

"But this was the first time you ever did the medal, right?"

"Yeah, but it was also the first time Ryan ever saw me ride. He probably doesn't even want to teach me anymore."

"Okay, now you're just being dramatic," Kaitlyn said, dunking a piece of her pretzel into a little container of caramel sauce. "Oh, guess what I heard from my neighbor who rides with Ava? She's got some big show coming up and then after that she's quitting riding. She's done. Going to do gymnastics."

"Maybe I should take up gymnastics, too. Or tennis, or competitive Ping-Pong, or anything else but riding," Tally said, a smile tugging at the corner of her mouth. Even she had to admit she sounded ridiculous.

"Stop!" Kaitlyn shouted at her, flicking a little pile of pretzel salt in her direction. "Let's round out this dinner with some ice cream. I'm buying to cheer you up."

And it actually worked. While Tally enjoyed a waffle cone filled with soft serve and sprinkles (how could that *not* put you in a better mood?) Kaitlyn chatted about the older boys in school she thought were cute and how she hoped one of them would take her to the eighth-grade dance later that fall.

To Tally, seventh grade was such a weird time—almost like she felt caught between being a child and being a teenager. The idea of trying to get a seventh or eighth grader to invite her to the dance made her skin crawl. Most of them were just gross, and some were downright mean to the girls, or to anyone who didn't fit into their group. She'd much rather ride, hang out at the barn, or go shopping with her girlfriends than talking about boys. The subject always made her feel left out.

CHAPTER 9

That Wednesday in school, Tally felt the dread building in her stomach with each passing class. Today would be her first lesson with Ryan and she was even more nervous than she'd been at the show. Now she had to prove to him that she didn't actually suck at riding as much as she had on Sunday. She'd had fresh start with her new trainer at the show—now she had a hole to dig out of to prove herself to him.

At lunch, Ava told Tally and Kaitlyn that she'd be leasing Danny out while she took a year off of riding to try gymnastics with her sister. Maybe even selling him if the right show home came along for the pony. She also showed her friends a bite mark on her leg—the result of being distracted while grooming.

"Ponies are mean, huh?" Tally asked with a laugh.

Ava looked thoughtful before she answered. "Honestly, I think they're just really smart. They're little and could get picked on by all the bigger horses, so they have to be clever. And they can have such attitudes. They teach little kids how to ride so they have to put up with a lot, which explains the attitude, I think. But that makes it feel even more amazing when you click with them and lay down a really great trip."

Once school was over, and Tally went up to the barn office that afternoon, she was relieved to find that she'd be riding Sweetie. At least she'd have that normalcy in what she expected to be an intimidating lesson. She brought Sweetie to the ring alongside Jordan and the big bay school horse, Harry. Ryan was already waiting for them up at the indoor.

"Go ahead and walk these horses around on a loose rein. Tally, Jordan, this is Mac, she'll be jumping in on your lesson today."

Mac walked past on Joey and gave Tally a little wave.

Once all three girls were mounted and had allowed their horses a couple of laps at an easy walk, Ryan told them to gather up their reins and establish some contact.

"Once you've let the horses meander around a little,

I want you to get them between your leg and your hand right away. Work on getting that slight inside bend in the corners. I know we're just walking here but we want to get the horses acclimated to working. Not overbent, Mac, don't let his head go past the vertical. Jordan, you're gonna need a lot more leg than that, keep after him."

Tally shortened her reins and closed her legs around Sweetie's sides, feeling the mare engage her hind end.

"Did you feel that, Tally?" Ryan asked, and Tally nodded, glancing down at Sweetie's rounded neck.

"Keep your eye up and keep feeling what's going on under you. I'm glad you felt her engage like that. Now go ahead and everyone pick up your posting trot. Tally, hold that contact in your transition."

Keeping her hands still and eyes up, Tally signaled the mare to trot, holding the contact through her reins while maintaining her deep heels and calves tight on the mare's barrel. Sweetie lifted her head briefly and Tally felt her back hollow, just for a second, before accepting the contact again and staying round.

"Good!" Ryan said. "Work on keeping that as you trot around here. Inside leg to outside rein."

The riders trotted on the rail and on smaller circles as they eased into the lesson.

"Now, Tally and Jordan, stand up into your two-point," Ryan called out to them. "Mac, go right to sitting trot and drop your stirrups."

As the horses went around, Ryan set up some jumps, glancing up at each rider periodically.

"Tiring, right?" he asked after they'd done a few laps. "Stay up in your two-point though. Don't get fatigued in that core, this is how we get you strong for the equitation. For all your riding. You're gonna feel tired but your muscles are getting really strong."

Across the ring, Tally noticed Mac's pony dropping down to the walk from his formerly collected trot. Of course, Ryan saw it too.

"That never happened," said Mac playfully as she squeezed the pony back into a trot.

"Ok, I'll give it to ya," Ryan replied, winking when he caught Tally's eye.

After what felt like an hour of trotting in two-point, Ryan asked everyone to walk and catch their breath. The sensation in Tally's core reminded her of sleepover parties where she and her friends had laughed so hard that their stomach muscles hurt. The horses and ponies walked another lap or two before cantering in both directions.

"Let's do this little exercise in the middle here, going away from home," Ryan called to them. "It's a rail, an X, and then another rail—just a bounce in between each."

Tally found herself first to go and made the turn too early, eager to get to the exercise. Sweetie cantered through it easily.

"Were you straight?" Ryan asked.

"No."

"I can't teach you to jump a course of fences if you can't get straight to rails on the ground and a tiny X. Everyone keep coming."

Oof, there it was. The Ryan she'd been expecting. But instead of feeling discouraged, all Tally wanted to do was improve the exercise the next time and show Ryan she could do it.

She concentrated on keeping Sweetie straight down the long side and waiting to make the turn. The mare was a lot straighter this time as they approached the rail.

"Better," Ryan called. "Now right leg, right leg,

don't let her drift...that's fine. This next time through, let's work on your body. You don't need to lie on the neck here, it's just a little cross rail."

Mac and Joey were far enough ahead that Tally watched them canter through the exercise. Mac was up slightly out of the saddle and her arm softly followed the pony's mouth as he cantered through the bounces.

"Did you see that?" he asked Tally.

Was there anything this guy didn't notice? Tally nodded her head yes.

"Hold your body like that."

The next time through, Tally tried to copy what she'd seen Mac do.

"Ok, now you're just stiff and posing. Walk a minute. Mac, catch the exercise and then turn left to the oxer at the end of the ring. Tally, I want you to watch Mac's upper body. Jordan, you too."

The girls watched as Mac guided Joey through the exercise again, turning her head to the left over the cross rail, and then cantering down to the oxer.

"Watch how it's different now," Ryan said after the bounce exercise, and Tally automatically counted Mac and Joey's last few strides in her head before the oxee:

three, two, one, jump. As Joey took off, Mac sunk down into her heels, her hands following his mouth and her upper body closing at the hip. They landed off the oxer and within a couple of strides, she slowed him to a walk.

"Over the little exercise, her position didn't change much, right?" Ryan asked them. "She allowed with her hand and just held her body still. There's no reason to duck down to the neck and throw the reins away at a teeny X. You just want to allow. Then at the oxer, she opened her knee angle a little bit more to stay with the pony for the bigger effort, being sure to follow his mouth again with her hand. Make sense?"

Jordan looked wide-eyed and maybe a little overwhelmed, Tally thought. She felt the same way, but she was also excited to try it herself.

"Try that same thing, Tally."

On the approach to the exercise, Tally thought about allowing with her hand, rather than just trying to copy Mac's body position or even thinking about her own upper body, really. She let her hand follow Sweetie as they went through the bounces, thinking only about keeping her leg on the mare to hold her straight.

"Good! Now keep going to the oxer."

Encouraged by the praise and excited to get to the next fence, Tally guided Sweetie to the left and they slowed down a bit in the turn.

"Why are you spinning her with that inside rein? Use your leg, Tally. The outside one. Push your horse over and keep your canter the same." In the time it took him to bark all those directions, Tally and Sweetie were just a few strides out.

"Three, two, one," she whispered to herself and bent at the hip as Sweetie took off to clear the oxer. Tally felt the mare's mane brush her chin as they flew over the fence. Her heels had been really deep too, and she hoped Ryan noticed.

"No, no! What did we just talk about with your body?" There was so much to remember, Tally felt like she couldn't keep track of it all. Jordan rode through the exercise and the oxer, her brown braid bouncing on her back, and her long legs still against Harry's sides. Then it was Mac's turn to go again, and Tally visualized herself riding the same way.

"Outside leg in the turn, hold your body up," Tally whispered to herself.

"One more time, Tal," called Ryan, and Tally picked

up her canter, reviewing the points in her head.

They bounced through the exercise, and she held her outside leg on Sweetie, holding contact through the right rein and keeping her inside aids softer than before.

"That's it! Now keep your leg on to maintain your rhythm and control your body at the oxer."

Tally exhaled as she rode through the turn and straightened out for the oxer.

Three, two, one, Tally thought and sunk down into her heels while opening up her knee angle. Sweetie's considerable effort over the oxer automatically closed Tally's hip angle to just where it needed to be, and she resisted the urge to duck down any lower. Sweetie landed off the jump and they navigated the turn past the in-gate.

"Nice, Tal! Did you feel the difference there?"

"Yes," Tally answered honestly, feeling more pride—and, frankly, more tired—than she ever remembered feeling after a lesson before.

· CHAPTER 10 ·

"So? What did you think?"

Mac brought Joey to a halt next to Sweetie at the wash stalls, clipping him onto the cross ties and giving him a pat on the neck. He nodded his head in Sweetie's direction and the mare pinned her ears. Her initial fascination with the new pony had obviously worn off.

"It was a great lesson," Tally answered honestly. "I can't believe how tired I am!"

"Really?" Mac said with a little tilt of her head. "Then I hate to tell you this, but it's only going to get harder. The more Ryan gets to know you, the harder the lessons get."

Tally thought back on the times she'd heard Ryan teaching Mac in the indoor. Compared to that, today had been a breeze.

"Hey, did you hear about Danny?"

"Ava's pony? Yeah, she told me in school that she was leasing him out for a year, or he may even get sold," Tally replied, still distracted by the thought of her lessons getting even harder.

"I think he's coming here. Ryan has a client looking for a pony. Wait until you see how cute this one is," Mac said with a dreamy look in her eye. It seemed like certain ponies had a reputation around the horse show crowd. Everyone seemed to know a lot about them even if they were from different barns.

Side by side, the girls sprayed down their animals— it was warm for October and both Sweetie and Joey seemed to be enjoying their outdoor showers.

"Hey, when are you showing next?" Tally asked. Oaks schooling shows were fun, but she was starting to feel curious about the away shows Mac talked about.

"I think on Saturday. You should come watch!"

"Yeah, that's what I was thinking. I'll ask my mom, but I'm pretty sure she'll say yes."

"We can pick you up," Mac offered, turning off the water on her side of the wash stalls and running a sweat scraper over Joey's coat. The pony appeared to be fully asleep.

"Great," Tally said, filling a bucket with shampoo and warm water. She started sponging Sweetie's legs and worked up to her neck and shoulder. The mare let out a big sigh and her eyelids looked heavy. As much as Sweetie had her grumpy-mare moments, she did love her spa treatments. She and Joey had that in common, but it didn't seem like there was much Joey *didn't* enjoy. He was like a big puppy to be around on the ground.

"Can I have your number? I'll text you the details when I get home—my mom always writes the show stuff down on our calendar on the fridge."

Tally smiled, nodded, and gave Mac her number. She couldn't imagine getting to compete so often that the details weren't top of mind. Any time an Oaks show came up, she basically had the horse show schedule memorized down to the class numbers off the prize list.

When they got back to Sweetie's stall, Tally let the mare nuzzle at her pockets in search of treats.

"You think it's in there?" she said with a laugh as the mare brushed her muzzle back and forth on Tally's left

♘

pocket. She fished out the treats and Sweetie eagerly scooped them up from her palm.

After a final snuggle, Tally left Sweetie's stall, put her tack away, and went upstairs to the office to start on her homework while she waited for her mom. Settling into the couch by the big windows and cracking open her history book, Tally was about to start on her reading when she heard Ryan's voice on the other side of the office. A partition wall divided the viewing area side from the staff side, where Marsha had a desk and the instructors would leave their things or take phone calls.

"I think that's a very reasonable goal for the upcoming show season," Ryan was saying on the phone. He had some one-word answers for the person on the other end of the line, and Tally heard him mention something about Mac and Joey. She didn't mean to listen, but Ryan had one volume: loud. So this didn't really count as eavesdropping.

"Look, she's not necessarily the most naturally talented rider, but she puts in the time and tries really hard. She does her homework and it pays off. That makes her a contender."

☙

Tally was shocked by what she was hearing. Mac was an *amazing* rider. If that didn't come naturally, then Tally was even more impressed with the way she rode. Her dad's note flashed into her head.

HARD WORK BEATS TALENT WHEN TALENT DOESN'T WORK HARD.

All at once it made total sense to Tally. She and Mac both had to work hard, just in different ways. Without a horse of her own, Tally had to work at the barn for extra rides, filling water buckets and pushing heavy bales of hay up and down the aisle. And now that she had a more difficult instructor, she had to push herself to try new things and really focus in her lessons. And Mac might have owned a fancy pony, but she had to put in the time in the saddle—maybe even more time than other riders—to move up and be competitive in the division.

Down in the indoor below the office, Tally watched a rider who couldn't have been more than six years old practicing the up-down-up-down of her posting trot on one of the more patient school ponies. The windows were open a crack in the office today so

Tally could hear the instructor down in the ring.

"Hard, isn't it?" the instructor asked. The little girl stopped her posting, a cue to the pony that he could immediately slow to a walk. The rider nodded her head yes, her face red from the effort.

Hard, Tally thought, *but worth it.*

· CHAPTER 11 ·

Tally could not stop staring. She'd never seen so many gorgeous horses and ponies in one place. Each one clipped and groomed to a shine, manes and tails braided in perfect, tight rows. The showgrounds, part of the campus of a private school with a well-known riding program, featured three rings that ran hunter, equitation, and jumper classes simultaneously. The jumps set up in each show ring were nearly as beautiful as the horses. At Oaks shows, jumps were just standards and rails, sometimes with a couple of flower boxes positioned on the ground below the bottom rail. Here, each jump was like a piece of artwork. Even the standards were beautiful—some were adorned with wagon wheels while others were shaped like wishing wells and pine trees. In the ring on the far end of the grounds, where the jumpers competed, there were standards shaped and painted like the wings of monarch butterflies.

"Which ring are you showing in?" Tally asked Mac. They had time before the Medium Pony Hunter division would begin, so Mac suggested they walk the show grounds and get some food.

"The indoor. Here, I'll take you inside to see it."

The girls walked up a soft gravel path and into the indoor ring. The jumps were brimming with brush and greenery. One jump appeared to be made up of *only* brush.

"Sweetie will jump anything but I think even she would look twice at that," Tally said with a laugh and a nod toward the brush.

"Yeah, we haven't jumped brush like that yet," Mac said, her eyes narrowing as she looked from the ring to the course diagrams posted just outside it. "Hopefully Joey doesn't think he's supposed to eat it. Or that I'm supposed to."

Joey and Mac would have a couple of opportunities at the brush, since this was a one-day show. In most A-rated shows, Mac had explained to Tally, a division was spread out over two days. But this was a local, one-day A show so all of the jumping classes of the division took place in a row.

Tally laughed and followed Mac out of the back door, stealing one more glance at the ring before they left. Giant ceiling fans turned lazily at the top of the cathedral ceiling. The walls were decorated with blown up photos of school alumni who'd gone on to major championships, from what Tally could gather. Many of the show or class names were acronyms, and while she didn't know what the letters stood for, she could easily see the perfect form of each horse and rider in the photos.

After a text to Ryan's groom, Lupe, to see what he wanted, the girls picked up their food (grilled cheese for Mac, quesadilla for Tally, and a Coke for Lupe) and walked over to the trailer where Joey was waiting.

"Do ponies get scared alone on the trailer?" Tally asked.

"Some do, some don't. But Joey's on there with Danny. That new girl is trying him at the show today. So they'll keep each other company."

Mac had walked the show grounds fully dressed

to compete, except for her show coat and number, so the first order of business was for her to put those on when the girls arrived at the trailer.

"You ready for him, Mac?"

"Yes, thanks, Lupe," Mac said, handing him the can of Coke.

"Gracias," Lupe replied, giving her a quick fist bump. He led Joey off the trailer while Mac ate a few bites of her lunch, centered her number on her back, and threaded the shoe string through one of her button holes. Tally noticed that she was doing everything just so, making things perfect, then double-checking them before moving on.

Off the trailer, Joey held his head high, looking around at the new surroundings. He then lowered his head all the way to the ground and blew hard, as if he were suspicious of the grass away from home.

"Do you leave the earplugs in, Mac?"

"Yeah, leave 'em. Thanks, Lupe."

Just as Tally was wondering why a pony would need earplugs, Mac seemed to read her mind.

"It keeps him a little more quiet and focused when he's not distracted by every little sound," Mac told

Tally as she straightened her helmet on her head, feeling around for any flyaway hairs.

In what seemed like a matter of seconds, Lupe had the pony fully tacked up and handed the reins to Mac.

"Head on over," he said. "Ryan will be in the schooling ring."

Tally followed Mac toward the ring, absentmindedly petting Joey on his gleaming shoulder.

"He really looks amazing."

"Aw thanks, Tal. I'm glad that elbow grease is paying off!"

Tally remembered seeing the term "elbow grease" in a recent issue of one of her riding magazines. She made a mental note about it as they arrived at the schooling area.

Mac brought Joey to a stop in front of a mounting block placed just outside the ring. She swung her leg over her saddle like it was any other day and walked off. The two of them looked like such pros to Tally, completely at ease among all the frenetic activity. In the ring, Ryan was laughing with another trainer as they set a plain white vertical in the middle of the ring for another horse and rider. Mac walked Joey a bit around the ring which was bordered by tall pine trees, before picking up an easy trot.

Sitting down at a picnic bench right outside the ring, Tally took in the chaos of horses and ponies warming up. Everyone was going in different directions and seemed to have separate agendas. She even witnessed a near-crash between two horses. Their riders grumbled a bit but just kept on riding as though it were no big deal. Mac and Joey, trotting in the other direction now, looked completely unfazed by the circus around them.

"Hey Mac, go ahead and canter a couple laps on a loose rein and then we'll jump a little, okay?"

After Mac had Joey warmed up in both directions, Ryan stood to one side of that vertical in the center of the ring and watched them jump it off the left lead.

"Good," Ryan said. "That's the canter you want. That's ring speed. Go ahead and jump this down the hill a couple of times now off your right lead, keeping that pace the same."

Mac sat up a little taller going to the right, balancing Joey as he cantered down to the vertical. Ryan had raised the top rail a few holes. To Tally, the jump was now set at an intimidating height.

"Good!" Ryan said when Joey landed. "Let's go."

The three of them walked out of the ring and Ryan held up his hand to give Tally a high five. "Hey, spectator. Good for you, coming to watch. You can learn a lot by just watching at a horse show."

"I love it," Tally answered honestly. She hadn't thought much about learning so much as finally getting to see one of these big shows she always read and heard about.

"Just a second, girls."

Tally gave Joey a pat and looked up at Mac. "Ryan is nice at shows!" she said with a giggle.

"There isn't really much you can do here in terms of schooling, so I think he just wants to keep your confidence up and keep it fun," Mac said with a shrug. "You just want to get a couple decent distances in the schooling area before you go in. The work happens at home, you know?"

Before Tally could answer, a rider who appeared to be their age was leading Danny, whose ears were pinned, toward the schooling ring. Ryan stopped to face her.

"Sophia, right?"

The girl nodded.

"Turn around and take that pony back to the trailer.

His tail is full of shavings. I know you are new to this program, but we bring our horses to the ring spotless."

Tally felt a wave of embarrassment for this new rider, but the girl's expression looked more annoyed than upset.

"And while you're down there, fix your hairnet. The sides need to be pulled up along your hairline. I shouldn't be able to see the hairnet elastic on either side of your face. One of my many pet peeves."

"I didn't see a groom down at the trailer to take care of the pony's tail," Sophia replied, her voice a bit haughty.

"I'm sorry?" Ryan looked more than a little angry. "Let me tell you right now: This isn't going to be the right match if you can't do something as simple as picking shavings out of a pony's tail and putting your hairnet and your helmet on properly."

With a barely-detectable roll of her eyes, Sophia turned on her heel, pulling Danny behind her back to the trailer. *Whoa. So much for nice, easygoing Ryan at the shows.* Mac looked unbothered by the exchange as she nudged Joey forward and gestured for her to follow them. Tally wasted no time in keeping up with Mac and Joey after such an awkward exchange.

The more Tally hung around, the more she learned about Ryan and the way he did things at Field Ridge, the name of his business that he ran out of Oaks. She still wasn't quite sure what to make of it.

After watching a few of the other medium ponies go in the indoor, it was Joey and Mac's turn to jump the first course.

"In for their first hunter trip, this is number 440: Smoke Hill Jet Set, with Mackenzie Bennett in the irons."

Fancy announcer, Tally thought to herself as she watched her friend enter the ring and pick up a trot. Joey swept across the ground like he did at home. He had his ears pricked forward and a little extra spring in his step. It looked like he enjoyed being at a horse show.

After bringing Joey down to a walk for just a few steps, Mac picked up a canter and off they went. Joey maintained that forward canter they'd practiced and Tally held her breath as they approached the first jump, hunting it down together. Joey snapped his knees up and made a pretty, round effort over that first fence, and the seven fences that followed. Tally noticed one quiet distance into a line but Mac somehow made it look easy to cover the ground and Joey stretched for the oxer at the end of the line.

"Not bad at all for your first trip, Mac!" Ryan said, patting the pony as the pair walked out of the ring. Just keep your leg on through the turn to that out-side line, and the jump in will come up better. Then you can sit up and balance down the line rather than pushing to get out."

Mac nodded and Tally noticed that same, steely expression in her eyes that she often saw while Mac was in the saddle.

"You know your second course?"

Mac did know it, and she rode it even better than the first. They jumped the brush in their second trip and Tally watched as Joey's ears flicked back at Mac a few strides out, as if he were checking in with her about this different-looking obstacle. But she kept him on track and they jumped it without a problem.

"Whoooo hooo!" Ryan hollered at the end of their trip. Tally joined him in applauding. Mac walked Joey out of the ring, and scratched his neck affectionately.

Their third course, which the announcer called the handy, was their best one yet. They scored an 80. Mac wasn't quite as consistent with her canter rhythm, so they found another quiet distance or two, but the course was still quite good overall. Better than Tally could do, she thought, in awe of her friend. Ryan cheered again and Mac leaned down over Joey's neck to give him a hug.

When there were only a couple trips left in the division, Mac took off Joey's martingale and Lupe took off his saddle, setting it on the fence line inside the ring and wearing the martingale over his shoulder. The announcer came on the PA with the order of the jog, which designated where the ponies pinned, provided they jogged soundly. Joey was fourth in the first trip, then third, and another third in the handy. Tally looked at Mac's face when the results were announced and detected a hint of a smile before that look of determination took over again as Lupe reset Joey's saddle for the hack.

Tally watched the dozen-or-so ponies in the division as they trotted and cantered around the ring. Many of them moved like Joey: big, sweeping strides at the trot, and straight front legs at the canter. That canter movement reminded Tally of the Rockettes she once saw in New York City with her parents.

"Walk, please, all walk, and line up in the center of

the ring with your numbers facing the judge."

A pretty gray pony named Sunbriar Symphony was called first to collect the blue ribbon. "Second place," continued the announcer, "goes to Smoke Hill Jet Set, ridden by Mackenzie Bennett."

Tally watched as Ryan walked out of the ring, breaking into a big smile as a woman in the ring handed Mac a red ribbon. Just outside the ring, Ryan reached over Joey's neck and hugged Mac, slapping her on the back. "Nice job, Mac. Solid rides, lots of improvement."

Mac smiled broadly and gave Joey another big pat. She jumped off and wrapped Joey's neck in a hug before handing the reins to Lupe. Tally heard Mac whisper to her pony, "Thank you, my good boy."

Tally was so happy for Mac and for Joey, but there was another thought that had been nagging at her while she watched her friend go around.

And as hard as Tally tried to shake the thought, it just lingered in her mind like an unwelcome visitor, demanding her attention. *Would she ever have the right horse, and the ability herself, to compete in a show like this one?*

CHAPTER 12

"So how was that big horse show?" Tally's dad asked over dinner a couple of nights later.

"It was awesome, I hope I can ride in a rated show like that someday. But I'm not sure about Ryan, he can be so tough."

"How so?" her mom asked, setting a large bowl of salad down on the kitchen table and joining Tally and her dad.

"Well, there was this new girl trying a pony at the show, and right when she got to the schooling area, Ryan yelled at her in front of everyone for not picking the shavings out of the pony's tail."

"So that's like a grooming thing?" her dad asked. Tally nodded. "That doesn't seem so mean to me. There's a way that things need to be done. And at a horse show, especially, don't they need to be really clean?"

"Yes, but Ryan was just so...picky. He also told her it was one of his pet peeves when a rider doesn't tuck her hairnet up into her helmet properly," Tally added. Her father looked thoughtful for a moment.

"I don't know, Tal. I think if you want to compete at a high level like this, you've got to pay attention to details. It sounds like that's what Ryan is doing. There's a saying, 'Take care of the little things and the big things will take care of themselves.'"

Sometimes her father could be so annoying. Tally thought back to the exchange between Ryan and Sophia...and the news that Mac later delivered that the girl decided not to lease the pony and ride with Ryan after all. No one who saw what happened at the show, and Sophia's generally stuck-up attitude, was surprised to hear this.

"Come on, Dad, you mean that if I put my hairnet on the right way then all my distances to the jumps will come up?"

"That's a little oversimplified, but ultimately, yeah. If you pay attention to all the little things—on and off the horse—overall, I would think that your competitions will turn out better. If you take care of your horse's grooming and your appearance properly, then Ryan won't have an issue with this stuff and everyone can warm up without getting stressed and upset. Right?"

"That's a really good point, honey," Tally's mom said to her dad, serving both of them salad. Much as Tally wasn't a fan of admitting that her parents were right...this time they were. It did make sense to take care of the little things, especially at a rated show. And that Sophia girl obviously had a bad attitude as well.

The next day, Tally went to the tack shop situated just outside the school side of the barn. She'd been thinking about what Ryan said about presentation. And she was always reading in her magazines about horses gleaming as the result of lots of elbow grease. She may not have a fancy show horse yet, but she could definitely pay more attention to Sweetie's coat and make the mare look her absolute best.

Tally had a twenty-dollar bill from her grandparents from her last birthday tucked into one of the front pockets of her breeches (she always saved her cash for horse purchases). She opened the door to the tack shop, a strip of bells on the door cheerfully announcing her arrival. The lady who worked there was helping a younger kid and her mom select a helmet, so Tally started browsing the grooming and horse care sections herself.

She scanned the shelves for several minutes but came up empty.

"I'm back, Jean!" someone called from the doorway.

"Go ahead and help that girl over there, would you, please?"

"Hi," said the younger woman who'd just walked into the tack shop. "Can I help you find something?"

"Hi, yes," Tally replied. "I'm looking for elbow grease."

The saleswoman flashed her a quick smile, and then looked mildly confused.

"I'm sorry, did you say elbow grease?"

"Yes, I've been reading about how much it helps horses' coats. Do you have it?"

The woman paused again, and for just a second, Tally wondered if the woman hadn't heard of it, and she'd have to find it somewhere else.

"Oh, sweetie, that's just an expression. It means to put a lot of effort into grooming your horse," the saleslady began. Tally felt her cheeks go hot. *An expression?*

"I can show you where our grooming supplies are—currycombs and mitts, brushes, things like that?"

"No, that's okay, thanks," Tally mumbled, hurrying out of the store as quickly as she could, thoroughly embarrassed.

Once inside the barn, she grabbed her grooming box from the tack room and rushed down the aisle to Sweetie's stall, as if she could outrun the humiliating memory.

"Hey girl," she said and Sweetie raised her head from her hay in response. Tally plopped the box down against the wall and the mare looked at it quizzically.

"So, I found out today that elbow grease is just an expression for putting a lot of work into your grooming. There's no actual grease," she told Sweetie, who had lost interest by now and was back to munching on her hay. There wasn't much that motivated the mare more than food. "Okay then. You keep eating and I'm going to get started on making you shine."

Twenty minutes of currying and brushing later, Tally led Sweetie to the outdoor ring, looking back at the horse on their walk up the hill and not seeing much shine in her coat. Clearly this was going to take more than one inspired grooming session, but Tally was up to the challenge.

"Go right to the sitting trot, girls, and drop your stirrups," Ryan called out once the horses had walked and trotted a couple of laps. Wednesday lessons were now just Mac and Tally. "Don't balance on your hands, Tal, your legs are stronger than that. There. Now shift forward at your hips so you're not behind the motion. Good. Hold that there. Both of you keep going at that sitting trot on a twenty-meter circle. Stay strong through your core to hold your body up."

Tally felt the sweat drip down her forehead, getting absorbed into her helmet liner. Her tall boots were finally starting to break in a little more at least. She wasn't sure she could deal with painful boots on top of everything else in Ryan's lessons.

"Finish this last circle that you're on, and once you get to the long side, pick up your canter. I don't want to see any shoving with your seat or bouncing around in the saddle when you do. Sink down, hold your position and put that outside leg on in a firm signal to your horse or pony to tell them what you want."

Ryan watched as Tally picked up the canter,

thankfully one of the easier things to do on Sweetie. "Keep your heel down and your toe forward, as if you had your stirrups," he told her. Then he turned his attention to Mac.

"When you throw your hands up the neck, does he go forward? No. Sit down but sit light, don't drive with your seat."

"Now, both of you, I'm gonna close my eyes and you tell me when you're at ring speed. Tally, that's the canter you need when you're cantering around a course at a show."

The girls worked on establishing ring speed, a newer concept to Tally, for the next few minutes, and then let their horses walk for a bit. Next they worked on collecting and extending the canter down a line of rails on the ground, set so that it could be ridden in five or six strides.

"You were a big fish in a small pond before, weren't you, Tally?" Ryan said to her when she failed to get down the outside line in the five. Again. She remembered a lesson with Meg when they did this exercise over small cross-rails. She couldn't get the strides consistently then either, but she felt like she'd made a solid attempt.

"I bet you were the best in your lessons. And that's

great. But you're swimming with the big fish now. I know you can do better. Both of you walk a minute while I set some jumps."

Tally had read about how jumping rails on the ground could be more difficult than navigating actual fences. The writer of that article had been correct. Much like her father, she thought bitterly. Doing so well in her lessons with Meg was "a sign that it's time to push yourself harder to get to that next level," her dad had told her. Guess he'd been right.

After Sweetie and Joey had a chance to catch their breath, Ryan set up a small, equitation-style course for the girls to jump: They would begin cantering downhill to the single coop, make a left turn to the natural diagonal, inside turn to the three-stride line, left turn to a diagonal single, right turn down the hill again to a single oxer. Then they had to halt, then turn right and trot up the hill over the coop again to finish. Mac was set to go first.

"Please don't make me fall asleep at the first jump," Ryan said dryly as Mac and Joey rounded the turn with a medium canter. Joey perked up when he saw the coop and they met the first jump well.

"All right, I'll take that."

Tally watched as the pair completed the course. Ryan went over some particulars with Mac as Tally reviewed the course in her head once more.

"Okay, Tal, you're up. But you only get to jump the course if you can get that five strides over the rails first. One shot. Don't mess it up or no course." He followed that up with a wink, but that didn't mean he wasn't serious.

"Pick up your canter and then establish the pace you want. Ring speed. Get that canter and keep her there. Then jump in and just keep kicking to get out in five. We'll work on finessing it, but for now, I just want you to get that number, so cowboy-kick if you have to."

As they approached the first rail, Tally felt like they were flying. Almost as if they were going too fast.

"That's the pace, Tal don't change it. Now jump in and count."

Sweetie took a big, leaping canter stride over the first rail. Before, Tally would relax and hope that the five would come up with the help of the big jump in. This time, she kept her leg on and trusted Ryan. It felt like *too* much pace, but it was worth a try.

"One, two, three, four, five! Nailed it, Tally! Now keep cantering and jump your course."

Tally continued down the long side, stifling a smile at finally accomplishing the five strides, and steered Sweetie toward the coop, which they flew over. Tally gathered her up for fence two, all while making sure that her rhythm didn't change too drastically. They met the second fence right out of stride and Sweetie made another good effort while Tally remembered to hold up her upper body and not collapse on Sweetie's neck.

"Ah ha!" Ryan declared. "See how the jumps come up when you maintain that ring speed?"

The rest of the course went well. One distance was a little long while another was quiet, but both acceptable, Tally thought. She missed a lead change but they had a good, clean halt, and Sweetie kept trotting all the way to the base of the last fence before popping over and cantering away with a happy little shake of her head.

"Not bad," Ryan told them with a serious nod. "See you next week."

· CHAPTER 13 ·

During Tally's next working student shift at the barn, the temperature had dropped considerably. She ran into Kaitlyn, who had a lesson that afternoon, and borrowed her jacket. It was a lot cooler working on the aisle than it was riding.

When it was time to fill the water buckets on the boarders' aisle, Tally popped in her ear buds to finish up the work. She liked to get in the zone sometimes during her shifts, thinking about what she was working on in her lessons as she went about her barn chores. This felt far too nerdy to admit to anyone so she kept that little factoid to herself.

Ryan and his clients had really settled in to the boarders' side of the barn. Field Ridge was embroidered on the tack trunk covers and horse coolers, all of which were hunter green. Once she'd finished about half the boarder aisle, Tally noticed someone appear outside the tack room. She took out one of her earbuds and looked up to see Ryan waving at her from the doorway.

"Hey," he said, walking toward the stall where she'd just finished watering. The horse inside bumped her with his muzzle and she gave him a pat. "I just wanted to see if you could do a little something for me during your shift."

"Of course, what is it?" Tally asked.

"That horse at the very end of the aisle...could you go in and put a good layer of elbow grease on him?"

Tally's mind went blank for a moment before realizing that Ryan was making fun of her. He winked and she turned a deep red. She scrambled to think of a response that wouldn't make her sound any more stupid, but Ryan wasn't done talking.

"I'm just having fun with you. My friend Ally works in the tack shop and she told me you went shopping for elbow grease. I actually think it's great that you take such an interest in horse care. Which is why I wanted to ask you if you'd groom and hop on a pony for me after your shift. So long as you'll cool him out well and slather on that special grease afterward."

"Sure!" Tally said, excited to have an extra ride. She didn't have any of her riding clothes and she'd have to make sure her mom could pick her up late, but she'd worry about all that later. "Which pony?"

"His name is Danny," Ryan said. "I have a new client who wants to use him as a children's pony for the kid to move up on, but I've only seen him go with his old owner. It would be helpful to get a better sense of how he goes. Think you can be on in the small indoor in twenty minutes?"

"Yes, no problem. Thanks, Ryan."

"Thank you," he said and walked off, leaving Tally to figure out all the pieces. She texted her mom, who agreed to pick her up later as long as she promised she wouldn't get behind on her homework, and Mac, who told Tally where to find her helmet and half chaps in her tack trunk. Luckily, both fit her...more or less.

Ryan had left Danny's tack outside his stall so she let herself in to brush him and pick out his feet. Danny immediately pinned his ears and went after her with his teeth. Not like Sweetie's pretend bite, either—this was a serious, open-mouthed attempt at taking a chunk out of her arm.

"Hey!" she said and raised her hand to back him off.

"He's less likely to bite you if you put him on the cross ties," a woman in gray breeches and tall boots said as she walked down the boarders' aisle.

"Thanks," Tally said tentatively, grabbing Danny's halter and avoiding another attack as she led him out of the stall to the cross ties.

Just inside of Ryan's twenty-minute timeframe, Tally had groomed and tacked Danny, only getting bitten lightly once on the leg, and made her way to the ring. She mounted up, immediately noticing how much of his barrel she could wrap her legs around, and wondering if she was a little on the tall side for ponies. Tally nudged Danny forward and pinned his ears again.

She walked a lap on a loose rein in the smaller indoor until Ryan came into the ring.

"Go ahead and trot him around, Tal. He needs a lot of leg, so don't be afraid to get after him a little. Make some circles, use all of the ring."

Tally did as Ryan asked. It wasn't easy to keep the

pony moving forward. Danny was sulky at the in-gate and whenever the other horse in the ring occupied space in the same zip code as him. But when Tally thumped him with her heels he responded, and she was rewarded with a nice forward trot that felt as floaty and dreamy as it looked. Even if it made it harder to hold her position as he moved underneath her.

"Canter a little, Tal," Ryan called. It was surprising to Tally at first that he wasn't saying much. But this wasn't a lesson for her, it was just about him seeing the pony go.

It was easy to get the upward transition with just a squeeze—no more kicking—but Danny's canter was hard to stay with. He had such a huge stride that it literally felt like riding a rocking horse. At ring speed.

"A little different than riding Sweetie, huh?" Ryan asked her from the rail. "Try to sit lightly. If you perch up in a half seat he's just going to get strung out on his front end."

After some more cantering, Ryan adjusted the three-stride line on the diagonal to make it a rail on the ground followed by a small vertical.

"Pop up over this," he instructed her. "Canter in,

three strides from your rail to your vertical."

Danny cantered over the rail and Tally focused on the jump ahead. Danny was round through his neck so Tally was excited to see what his jump might feel like.

They cantered over the rail right out of stride. *Three, two, one*, Tally counted and Danny jumped the little vertical with a big, round effort, popping her out of the tack. She landed in a bit of a heap on the other side of the jump and watched him pin his ears again as they cantered away and she settled herself back into the saddle.

"That's all right, Tal, come get it again. Make sure you keep your leg."

This time around, Tally felt Danny suck back at the first rail, and three strides later, he ducked hard to the left. She lost her right stirrup and had a quick flash of panic that she was going to fall, but she recovered the stirrup and slowed Danny to a walk.

"He didn't trust you that time," Ryan said. "Come again and more leg. If you tell him to jump and you mean it, he should listen."

Tally tried to forget that the refusal ever happened as she turned around and came back to the exercise. A hard squeeze didn't get much reaction out of the pony, so she kicked Danny's sides and sat back in the saddle. They turned toward the rail and Tally held her left leg tight to his side. Maintaining her pace over the rail, Danny cantered the three strides and jumped the vertical hard again, with Tally grabbing mane this time to be sure she stayed with him.

"One more time, Tal," Ryan called, and Tally guided the pony around and went through the exercise again successfully.

"Good," he said, as Tally walked and patted the pony on his neck. "That's the right choice to grab some mane while you get used to his jump."

Get used to it? Tally thought with a twinge of excitement. *Would they be paired together again?* Ryan walked out of the ring without any further comment and Tally took her time letting Danny cool out. They hadn't done a ton, but she wanted to be sure she took good care of him. As the pony walked with his neck outstretched, Tally's mind wandered, daydreaming about getting to ride Danny again.

CHAPTER 14

One day at school in early November, Tally, Kaitlyn, and Ava sat down together for lunch. The final schooling show of the series at Oaks had been the day before, and Tally was excited to tell her friends about her second-place finish in the medal.

She enthusiastically recounted the course for her friends over their sandwiches and chips. It was fun to have a trot jump and a couple of rollbacks and actually ride them well this time, as opposed to their mess of a first attempt at the medal. Ryan seemed pleased with the trip too, which made it even more exciting. And Sweetie got good ribbons in the low hunter classes as well, so Tally was riding her horse show high well into the school day. Ava asked how Danny was doing and Tally told her about getting to ride him for Ryan, and about his potential new owner who would start him in the children's. It occurred to Tally that she was talking about divisions and pony terminology that she hadn't even been aware of just a couple weeks prior.

The girls all laughed about how mean Danny could be on the ground, and Tally wondered if Ava missed him. But Ava was already wearing t-shirts printed with her gym's logo to school and pulling her hair back tightly into a bun with a sparkly headband that she said matched her leotard—it seemed like her mind was far away from riding.

At the barn that afternoon, Tally zipped up her tall boots, grateful for how easily they now creased around her ankles and behind her knees. She rode Scout in her lesson and then flatted Danny afterward. Ryan didn't ask her to do any jumping so she focused on lightly sitting that rocking horse canter.

"How would you feel about taking lessons on Danny?" Ryan asked her when their hack was done. Tally was thrilled, but knew she had to manage her expectations, too. At any point, Ryan's client could buy or start leasing Danny, and she wouldn't have the rides on him anymore. She promised herself to just enjoy the rides on Danny while she had them.

The next few lessons were exciting for Tally, to ride a pony who was so athletic and talented. The problem was that he was also super smart, and if she made a mistake, he would stop. They weren't particularly scary or dirty stops, more like running out, but it was frustrating all the same. The goal, Ryan had told her, was to make the pony more honest for his upcoming rider, who was pretty green, having only ridden for a couple of years.

"He's telling on you!" Ryan shouted as Tally overanalyzed the distance to a single oxer on a long approach and Danny opted to scoot off to the side. "Don't pick. Just keep riding him forward and let the jump come to you. Trust his canter and trust that you'll get there."

With each lesson, Danny stopped less and less as Tally rode more definitively. She even figured out how to sit his canter lightly and stay with him over the jumps. Grabbing mane had become a necessity of the past. They practiced bending lines in their most recent lesson, and Tally loved jumping in and looking for their track to the second jump off her eye.

Down on the boarders' aisle, Tally took Danny's bridle off and quickly replaced it with his halter, careful to avoid the pony's teeth. She could see him considering whether to bite her and ultimately deciding that she was too quick for him now. She smiled to herself, thinking that Danny wasn't exactly mean, but more misunderstood. He needed his space, and Tally did her best to give it to him.

"Hey!" Mac called to her, clipping Joey on the cross ties behind Danny. "Ryan said you're riding Danny really well."

"He did?"

"Yeah, he's not an easy pony. But don't sound so surprised, Tal, you ride well."

With the compliment still sinking in, Tally got to work on the sweat marks on Danny's girth area with a towel. "Manners, please!" she reminded him when he bared his teeth at her. Now that they were deep into the fall, the horses' coats were filling in more, and the sweaty areas didn't dry as easily on their own. Mac told Tally about the Big Equitation classes she'd been watching on live streams.

"We should watch them together," Mac suggested.

"I'd love that. Where are these shows?"

Mac explained to her about "indoors," and how

the "big eq" classes were basically the highest level of a rider's junior career—and sometimes ended up being the first step for kids who would go on to the big leagues in show jumping. Tally always made sure to record Grand Prix show jumping whenever it was televised, but watching these equitation classes sounded just as fun.

"Come on, let's put these guys away and watch in the tack room," said Mac. "Do you have time?"

Tally nodded and the girls tucked the ponies into their stalls and retreated to the boarder tack room. They sat on the floor with their backs against the tack trunks as Mac pulled her laptop out of her school bag.

"I was just watching this one Maclay Final from a couple years back that's still available to stream. It's got really good commentary," she said. "I'm about thirty trips in but we can just pick it up there. You didn't miss any awesome rounds."

"How many trips are there?"

"In a national final? Hundreds," Mac said without looking up from her screen. Tally thought back to what she'd learned about Pony Finals. At the highest level, it seemed like winning was only a possibility for a fraction of the competitors. Everyone else was there to put in a good round, not necessarily to chase a ribbon. That seemed very grown up to Tally. A lot more mature than she was, anyway. Half of the fun of horse showing *was* the ribbons!

But as the girls got to watching the Maclay Final, Tally forgot about all that. It was amazing to watch these riders navigate a course of enormous fences like they were just "speed bumps," as she'd heard some people call the 2'6" fences she usually jumped. The commentators talked about the horses' adjustability and the best riders' ability to make those adjustments look invisible.

When one rider easily navigated a bending line of a tight four strides to a very open six strides, both Mac and Tally whispered "wow," in unison. They glanced at each other and laughed.

"That was amazing," Tally said, her eyes glued to the screen.

"She makes it to the final work-off," said Mac. "Wait until you see that. They switch horses for it, and they have to do the work-off without trying the horses first."

"Wait, you've seen this before?"

"Yeah, but it's been a while. I could watch it over and over though."

Tally smiled at the idea that she wasn't the only one who could totally nerd out when it came to riding.

"Hey, girls."

Both Tally and Mac jumped a little bit as Ryan appeared in the doorway.

"So, Tally, what are you doing this weekend?"

"Um, homework, probably."

"Think you can fit a horse show in?"

"Sure! To watch?"

"Actually, I was thinking you could do the children's on Danny for me."

Tally's jaw practically dropped and she caught Mac's eye. Mac silently clapped her hands together, clearly excited about the idea.

"Mac is coming too, and a couple of other clients. I'll cover the shipping, since this would be kind of a favor you're doing for me. You'd just have to pay for entries and the day training rate. Do you want me to run those numbers by your parents and we can take it from there?"

"That would be great, thank you, Ryan. I'll make sure they say yes!"

"Good luck with that," Ryan replied dryly. "Hopefully they approve, and then I'll get you entered. I want you do the children's ponies, since that's the division this new kid wants to do. The fences will have a lot of fill, like at the show you came to watch, but they won't be any bigger than what you do in lessons. Probably a hole smaller actually. I'll give your parents a call and I'll see you soon, kiddo."

Tally said goodbye to Ryan before turning to Mac with about a hundred questions.

"Don't stress out about it," Mac concluded as she packed up her laptop. "It's just another horse show."

Not to me, Tally thought, but that seemed too pathetic to say aloud. Actually, Tally felt like she never knew when her next show would be, so they all felt super important. But Mac was right, stressing about it wouldn't make the pony go any better, and it definitely wouldn't make her ride better. She walked toward the parking lot mentally practicing what she'd say to her mom and repeating it to herself to commit it to memory. This horse show was going to be a dream come true, and it was just around the corner. Tally had to make sure that she could get there.

· CHAPTER 15 ·

"Ryan already called me," Tally's mother said as her daughter was just beginning her sales pitch for the show.

"Really? What did you say?"

"I said I'd need to run it by your father, and I'd call him back. It's expensive, Tally. The training fee and the entries are a lot more than what we're used to with Oaks shows. Let me see what Dad thinks."

That night at dinner, Tally was ready to start convincing her father to let her do the show but he beat her to the punch.

"Tal, I'm really proud of you for working so hard. It sounds like it's paying off with this trainer asking you to ride a pony that's going to be sold. I want you to do this show," he began, and Tally excitedly jumped up to hug him as hard as she could.

"But!" he began, laughing and hugging her back. "You're going to need to put in some work to earn it if these things keep up. For now, how about we make it your big Christmas present a month early. Deal?"

"Deal," Tally agreed happily.

During the week, Ryan let Tally flat Danny an extra time in addition to their last lesson together on Friday before the show on Saturday. Mac had mentioned that Ryan would probably take it easy on them right before a show and she was right. They worked on the flat and then jumped a couple of courses.

"Feeling good?" he asked Tally. She nodded. "You'll probably have a course like this tomorrow. A couple of singles and lines that are set for the ring pace that we've been practicing. Just keep your leg on and you'll be fine."

The next morning, Tally's alarm went off at 6 a.m. and she flew out of bed, having been awake for at least an hour already. This was it. An away show. An A-rated show. Just like she'd watched Mac do and wished to be a part of herself someday. And she was already getting to do it.

As she got herself dressed, Tally blew her nose and

tossed the tissue into her trashcan, right on top of her popsicle-stick picture frame. She peered down at it, thinking about how upset she'd been when Meg left, but how much she'd actually gained already in riding with a new trainer.

Wearing her tan breeches and show shirt, tucked in and accented with a black stretchy belt, Tally checked herself out in the mirror and smiled. It was fun to feel like she looked the part. She pulled her lucky socks over her breeches, and tugged a long-sleeved workout top on over her show shirt to keep it clean. She'd wear sneakers until it was time to put on her tall boots to warm up, she decided. Easier to keep them clean that way. After all, she'd stayed up late in the garage polishing them.

Mac's mom was driving both girls to the show, and they chatted excitedly the whole way there.

"Will the ponies be braided?" Tally asked, surprising herself that she hadn't thought to ask such a key question sooner.

"Braided? Yeah," Mac said, distracted momentarily by her phone. All of a sudden, Tally's excitement gave way to nerves. She hadn't needed to grab mane for a while to stay with Danny's big jump, but it was a nice security blanket knowing that she could. That wouldn't be an option today if the pony were braided.

When the girls arrived at the Field Ridge trailer, both ponies peeked out at them from their windows. Tally was struck by the distinctive scent of hoof oil. It even smelled like a special day.

"Hi, boys!" Mac said, waving to Danny and Joey. Tally could hardly believe how cute and fancy Danny looked when he was braided.

"Morning, ladies," said Lupe, who was holding a Coke in one hand and a walkie-talkie in the other. "Ryan is ready for Danny at the schooling ring."

Tally sprung into action getting her boots, show jacket, and helmet on, just as she'd watched Mac do at the last show. Mac produced her number, 885, while Lupe tacked up the pony. The show was held at the same facility as the last one, so Tally was relieved to know her way around at least a little bit.

"Don't forget to breathe, Tally," Mac said, taking the reins from Lupe and walking the pony toward the schooling area for her while Tally secured her hair under a hairnet as they walked, pushing the sides up to her hairline. She mounted at the same spot where

Mac had gotten on last time, but Tally felt none of the ease she'd seen in her friend.

The warm-up turned out to be pretty low key, with only a few other ponies in the ring. Danny flatted just fine and popped over the plain white jumps in the middle of the ring the same way he did at home. He clearly knew his way around the show grounds.

"Let's go look at your course," Ryan said, Tally's cue to follow him out of the ring. Ryan slowed down once they'd crossed through the open gate and gestured for her to bend down a bit to hear him.

"Black socks only, Tal. Needs to look professional," he said softly with a glance at her boots and then kept walking. Tally looked down to see green and cream horse shoes peeking out from underneath her boots. The embarrassment hit her like a punch. Things were not getting off on the right foot for her first big show.

"Hop off," Ryan said when they arrived at the posted course diagrams. Lupe appeared next to them and gestured to Tally that he'd hold the pony. Tally quickly unzipped her boots, scrunched her blue socks down her calves a few inches, and rezipped her boots.

"So, pretty simple for your first trip," Ryan began

as they faced the course diagrams near the in-gate together. This was Tally's first glance at the ring, and the jumps looked even more filled in and fancy than they did at the show where she had watched.

As Ryan talked her through the area of the ring where she should get Danny's canter up to speed, Tally fixated on the first jump. The standards were shaped like horse heads and there was a glossy, cream-colored rail with a cream gate below it, and flower boxes stuffed with fake red flowers and brush in front of that.

"Keep your leg on after that vertical and look left just a little bit so that he hopefully lands the lead. Then keep your canter through the turn and bring him back up to ring speed if you need to before the judges' line. Jump in and keep your leg for the six strides. He should walk right down it as long as you don't get in his face. They set the lines a little shorter in the children's so you won't be racing to get out."

Tally nodded as she cantered the course in her mind. She recognized the pine tree standards on the judges' line from the last show, and from the horse show pictures she always pored over online. Her mind started to wander as she daydreamed about actually being in the ribbons at this show, but she forced herself to keep taking in Ryan's instructions.

"Then you've got your diagonal line in seven strides. He's going to slow down here at the gate so you're going to really need that leg on, and thump him a little with your outside leg if you need to. Maybe I should have given you a spur. Well, let's see how he does in the first trip."

Tally felt embarrassed about possibly having to tell Ryan that she'd never ridden in spurs before, but they had to go over the rest of the course first. After the diagonal line, they would do the outside line in six, and then go all the way around to a single oxer coming home.

"Don't pick for that last distance, okay? Just let him canter on and the spot will show up, even if you don't see it right away."

Tally nodded and repeated the course to herself: vertical away from home off the right lead, judges' line, leg on for the diagonal line going away, outside line, long way around to the single oxer. *Let's just get over each jump, Danny*, she thought.

Ryan walked Tally around the perimeter of the ring so she could see what her approaches would look like.

They also watched a couple of ponies go and Tally could see how they sucked back by the gate and the riders had to move up to get the seven strides done up the diagonal line. One rider visibly kicked her pony for the last few strides where the other added and got eight strides.

"Ready?" Ryan asked. Tally felt like her heart was beating in her throat. She followed him toward the in-gate where Lupe was applying hoof oil to Danny's feet and Mac was wiping around his bit with a rag. Danny tried to bite her fingers and she swatted at his nose. Tally tightened the girth while Mac held Danny's face and Lupe pulled down the stirrups.

"On three," Ryan said, taking hold of Tally's shin. She hadn't gotten a leg up before but it seemed easy enough.

"One, two, three," Ryan lifted her shin from below, boosting up her whole body, and Tally clipped her right calf on the back of the saddle on her way up. Danny shifted grumpily.

"Let's do the course a little better than the mount, okay?"

Tally blushed and nodded, happy for a moment of comic relief. She couldn't believe how nervous she was as they walked right up to the in-gate. She also couldn't stop thinking about Danny stopping in her lessons and "telling on her," as Ryan put it. But fluttering in the wind just to their left was a wall of ribbons much more ornate than the ones they handed out at Oaks. Tally would have given anything to go home with one. Or maybe even more than one?

"Know your course, Tal?" Ryan asked as the rider in the ring cleared the last jump of her course.

"Right lead vertical, judges' line, leg on for the diagonal line, outside line, single oxer," Tally answered him.

"Good girl. Have fun."

Tally walked Danny into the ring and the pony instantly honed in on the greenery and flowers decorating the open area of the ring near the in-gate. She squeezed him with her heels and gathered up her reins for some contact. He flicked an ear back at her but still seemed a bit preoccupied with the flowers. Tally sat the trot to ask for the canter and remembered Mac's advice to breathe. Exhaling and sitting down into her saddle, she cued Danny for his right lead and he stepped into it seamlessly. Ryan stood with Lupe and Mac at the gate and nodded at her. Tally barely heard the announcer—"This is a first hunter trip for number 885, Stonelea Dance Party, ridden by Tally Hart"—as she focused on bringing Danny's canter up to ring speed and held her outside leg on him to shape the right turn toward the first jump.

Danny took three big strides out of the turn and then sucked back a bit, but Tally recognized this tendency in him from her lessons and squeezed him hard. He moved off her leg as they got closer to the first jump. Tally was relieved to see that the vertical didn't look any bigger than what they jumped at home, though it was decorated with even more flowers and filler than they could see from the in-gate.

Three, two, one, Tally counted to herself as they approached the take-off spot. But just as she started to think about opening her knee angle for the take-off, Danny dropped his head. Hard. He saw something he didn't like in those red flowers and the momentum of his ducking shot Tally's upper body forward, and onto his neck. Then, before she even realized what was happening, Tally got an up-close look at Danny's gorgeous braids as she jumped the cream and red vertical.

Without her pony.

The next few seconds were a blur as Tally ended up on the other side of the jump. She somehow managed to land on her hands and knees, and while she wasn't hurt, her pride was seriously wounded. Danny stood still on the other side of the vertical, one stirrup hanging down, the other flung up over his withers. The buckle of the reins was resting on the ground below the pony's head so Tally walked around the jump to scoop them up for safety's sake, even though Danny showed zero interest in going anywhere.

"You okay?" Ryan asked, appearing next to Danny and running the stirrups up the saddle.

"I'm fine," Tally said, adding quickly, "I'm really sorry."

"Don't be, it happens to the best of us," Ryan said with a wink. He helped her brush off the footing from the sleeves of her jacket and they walked out of the show ring together, with Ryan leading Danny and Tally trying her hardest not to cry as the spectators gave them a supportive round of applause.

At the gate, Mac mouthed "It's okay!" but Tally refocused her gaze down at her boots, polished in vain for her twenty seconds in the ring. *We didn't even get to jump one fence*, Tally thought miserably. Ryan asked an older, more experienced junior rider to get on Danny and do a schooling round in the show ring to get him over all of the jumps and end the day on a more productive note. Still fighting back tears, Tally watched their round from one of the benches just outside the fancy show ring, wondering if she'd ever have the chance to get back in it herself.

Keep reading the
***SHOW STRIDES* series!**

UP NEXT:

Confidence Comeback

Moving Up & Moving On

Testing Friendships

Packer Pressure

Always available at **theplaidhorse.com**

ABOUT THE AUTHORS

 Piper Klemm, Ph.D. is the publisher of *The Plaid Horse* magazine. She co-hosts the weekly podcast of The Plaid Horse, the #Plaidcast, and is a college professor. She has been riding since she was eight years old and currently owns several hunter ponies who compete on the horse show circuit. She frequently competes in the Adult Amateurs across North America on her horse of a lifetime, MTM Sandwich, so you might see her at a horse show near you!

FIND HER ONLINE AT piper-klemm.com
@ **@piperklemm**

 Rennie Dyball has loved horses for as long as she can remember. She began taking lessons at age twelve, was captain of the Penn State equestrian team, and now shows in the Low Adult hunters. Rennie spent fifteen years as a writer and editor at *People* and has co-authored more than a dozen books. Her picture book debut, *B Is for Bellies,* will be published by Clarion in 2023. With *Show Strides,* Rennie is delighted to combine two of her greatest passions—writing and riding.

FIND HER ONLINE AT renniedyball.com
@ **@renniedyball**

WHO'S WHO
AT QUINCE OAKS

Ava Foster: Friends with Tally and Kaitlyn, used to own Danny but quits riding.

Brenna: Barn manager at Quince Oaks

Field Ridge: Ryan's business within Quince Oaks

James Hart: Tally's dad

Jordan: Takes lessons at Quince Oaks, sometimes with Tally

Kaitlyn Rowe: Tally's best friend at school

Mackenzie (Mac) Bennett: Newcomer to the barn who owns Joey

Maggie: Takes lessons at Quince Oaks, sometimes with Tally

Marsha: the barn secretary at Quince Oaks

Meg: Tally's instructor at Quince Oaks before Ryan

Quince Oaks: The barn

Ryan McNeil: Mackenzie's trainer and Tally's new instructor after Meg leaves the barn

Scout: One of the Quince Oaks school horses

Smoke Hill Jet Set (Joey at the barn): Mac's medium pony hunter

Stacy Hart: Tally's mom

Stonelea Dance Party (Danny at the barn): Formerly Ava Foster's pony, goes up for sale through Ryan

Sweet Talker (Sweetie at the barn): Tally's favorite school horse

Tally (Natalia) Hart: Rides Ryan's sales ponies and in the lesson program at Quince Oaks

GLOSSARY OF HORSE TERMINOLOGY

A circuit: Nationally-rated horse shows.

base: Where a horse or pony leaves the ground in front of a jump; also: refers to the rider's feet in the stirrups, with heels down acting as anchors, or a base of support, for the rider's legs.

bay: A horse color that consists of a brown coat and black points (black mane, tail, ear edges, and legs).

canter: A three-beat gait that horses and ponies travel in—it's a more controlled version of the gallop, the fastest of the gaits (walk, trot, canter, gallop).

catch-riding: When a rider gets to ride and/or show a horse or pony for someone else.

chestnut: A reddish brown horse/pony coat color, with a lighter mane and tail.

chip: When a horse or pony takes off too close to a jump by adding in an extra stride near the base.

conformation class: A horse show class in which the animals are modeled and judged on their build.

cross-rail: A jump consisting of two rails in the shape of an X.

currycomb: A grooming tool used in circles on a horse or pony's coat to lift out dirt.

diagonal line: Two jumps with a set distance between them set on the diagonal of a riding ring.

distance: The take-off spot for a jump. Riders often talk about "finding distances," which means finding the ideal spot to take off over a jump.

flower boxes: Like "walls," these are jump adornments that are placed below the lowest rail of a jump.

gate: Part of a jump that is placed in the jump cups instead of a rail. Typically heavier than a standard jump rail so horses and ponies can be more careful in jumping them so as not to hit a hoof.

gelding: A castrated male horse.

girth: A piece of equipment that holds the saddle securely on a horse or pony. The girth attaches to the billets under the flaps of the saddle and goes underneath the horse, behind the front legs, and is secured on the billets on the other side.

green: A horse or pony who has less training and/or experience (the opposite of a "made" horse or pony, which has lots of training and experience).

gymnastic: A line of jumps with one, two, or zero strides between them (no strides in between jumps is called a bounce—the horse or pony lands off the first jump and immediately takes off for the next without taking a stride).

hack: Can either mean riding a horse on the flat (no jumps) in an indoor ring or outside; or, an under saddle class at a horse show, in which the animal is judged on its performance on the flat.

hands: A unit of measurement for horse or pony heights. One hand equals 4 inches, so a 15-hand horse is 60 inches tall from the ground to its withers. A pony that's 12.2 hands is 12 hands, 2 inches, or 50 inches tall at the withers.

handy: A handy class in a hunter division is meant to test a horse or pony's handiness, or its ability to navigate a course. Special elements included in handy hunter courses may include trot jumps, roll backs, and hand gallops.

in-gate: Sometimes just referred to as "the gate," it's where horses enter and exit the show ring. Usually it's one gate for both directions; sometimes two gates will be in use, one to go in and the other to come out.

jog: How ponies and horses in A-rated divisions finish each over fences class; the judge calls them to jog across the ring to check for soundness and orders the class. During the COVID-19 pandemic, the closing circle trot was used in place of the jog.

large pony: A pony that measures over 13.2 hands, but no taller than 14.2 hands.

lead changes: Changing of the canter lead from right to left or vice versa. The inside front and hind legs stretch farther when the horse or pony is on the correct lead. A lead change can be executed in two ways: A simple lead change is when the horse transitions from the canter to the trot and then picks up the opposite canter lead. In a flying lead change, the horse changes their lead in midair without trotting.

line: Two jumps with a set number of strides between them.

Maclay: One of the big equitation or "big eq" classes for junior riders. Riders compete in regional Maclay classes to qualify for the annual Maclay Final. The final is currently held at the National Horse Show at the Kentucky Horse Park in the fall.

mare: A mature female horse.

martingale: A piece of tack intended to keep a horse or pony from raising its head too high. The martingale attaches to the girth, between the animal's front legs, and then (in a standing martingale) a single strap attaches to the noseband or (in a running martingale) a pair of straps attach to the reins.

medium pony: A pony taller than 12.2 hands, but no taller than 13.2 hands.

outside line: A line of jumps with a set number of strides between them set on the long sides of the riding ring. An outside line set on the same side of the ring as the judge's box/stand is called a judge's line.

oxer: A type of jump that features two sets of standards and two top rails, which can be set even (called a square oxer) or uneven, with the back rail higher than the front. A typical hunter over fences class features single oxers as well as oxers set as the "out" jump in lines.

pinned: The way a horse show class is ordered and ribbons are awarded, typically from first through sixth or first through eighth place (though some classes go to tenth or even twentieth place).

Pony Finals: An annual show, currently held at the Kentucky Horse Park, in which ponies who were champion or reserve at an A-rated show are eligible to compete.

posting trot: When a rider posts (stands up and sits down in the saddle) as the horse or pony is trotting, making the gait more comfortable and less bouncy for both the rider and the animal.

regular pony hunter division (sometimes called "the division"): A national or A-rated horse show division in which small ponies jump 2'3", medium ponies jump 2'6", and large ponies jump 2'9"–3'.

rein: The reins are part of the bridle and attach to the horse or pony's bit. Used for steering and slowing down.

sales pony/sales horse: A pony or horse that is offered for sale; trainers often market a sales horse or pony through ads and by showing the animal.

school horses/school ponies: Horses or ponies who are used in a program teaching riding lessons.

schooling ring: A ring at a horse show designated for warming up or schooling.

schooling shows: Unrated shows intended for practice as well as for green horses and ponies to gain experience.

small pony: A pony that measures 12.2 hands and under.

spurs: An artificial aid, worn on a rider's boots to add impulsion.

stirrup irons: Also referred to as stirrups, the metal loops in which riders place their feet.

stirrup leathers: Threaded through the stirrup bars of the saddle and through the stirrups themselves; the leathers hold the stirrups in place.

tack: The equipment a horse wears to be ridden (e.g. saddle, bridle, martingale).

tall boots: The knee-high, black leather boots that hunter/ jumper/equitation riders wear with breeches when they reach a certain height or age. Prior to that, riders wear paddock boots (which only reach past the ankles) and jodhpurs with garter straps.

trail rides: A ride that takes places out on trails instead of in a riding ring.

transition: When a horse or pony moves from one gait to another. For example, moving from the canter to the trot is a downward transition; moving from the walk to the trot is an upward transition.

trot: A two-beat gait in which the horse or pony's legs move in diagonal pairs.

tricolors: The ribbons awarded for champion (most points in a division) and reserve champion (second highest number of points in that division).

trip: Another term for a jumping round, or course, mostly used at shows, as in, "the pony's first trip."

vertical: A jump that includes one set of standards and a rail or rails set horizontally.

THE PLAID HORSE

ENCOURAGES EVERY EQUESTRIAN TO:

READ   *The Plaid Horse* magazine
In print and online at
theplaidhorse.com/read

Subscribe at **theplaidhorse.com/subscribe**

READ   *With Purpose: The Balmoral Standard*
by Carleton Brooks and Traci Brooks
with Rennie Dyball

Available at **theplaidhorse.com/books**

READ   The re-release of
*Geoff Teall on Riding Hunters, Jumpers and
Equitation: Develop a Winning Style*

Available at **theplaidhorse.com/books**

LISTEN   The #Plaidcast
The podcast of *The Plaid Horse* at
theplaidhorse.com/listen

On Horse Radio Network, Audible, Spotify,
Apple Podcasts, Google Play, and Stitcher

LEARN   Explore your college credit
                education opportunities at
                theplaidhorse.com/college

LEARN   Attend the 6-12 grade fully accredited
                American Equestrian School
                americanequestrian.school

ENGAGE   Find out about local events
                featuring Piper & Rennie
                at **theplaidhorse.com**

FOLLOW   *The Plaid Horse* on social media:

                f Facebook.com/theplaidhorsemag
                🐦 Twitter @PlaidHorsemag
                📷 Instagram @theplaidhorsemag
                📌 Pinterest @theplaidhorsemag

NORTH AMERICA'S HORSE SHOW MAGAZINE • PUBLISHED SINCE 2003

Available at **theplaidhorse.com/books**

GOOD BOY, EDDIE
By Rennie Dyball

CHAPTER 1: New Barn

Up, FLOP. Up, FLOP. Up, FLOP.

"That's it, you're starting to get it: Up, down. Up, down. Up, down. That's how you post the trot," says the instructor. "But try to sit more lightly on Eddie and not come crashing down like a sack of potatoes, okay?"

I'm teaching my first lesson at New Barn and things are going pretty well. I am a school horse, and it's my job to teach people how to ride. The instructor, Melissa (she's the person who teaches the lesson with me), is standing in the middle of the ring while I trot around her in a big circle. The way my rider flops down in my saddle doesn't hurt, it's just a little uncomfortable. But I can tell that she's new to riding, so it's fine with me.

We go around and around the ring. There are walls on every side to keep the wind out. Wooden beams crisscross the high ceiling and I think I can see some birds' nests tucked up in the corners. Before I came here to this New Barn, I taught lots of riding lessons at a place much bigger than this one. I was one of about fifteen school horses back at the Old Barn. I had so many riders I eventually lost count! I really liked it back at Old Barn and I'm not sure why I had to leave, especially because I thought I was good at my job.

My new rider—Melissa keeps saying "Kennedy," so I suppose that's her name—was very nice to me in my stall when we were getting ready for the lesson, chatting the whole time. She smelled like soap and flowers. I don't know exactly what she was talking about, but she had a lot to say. And I was happy to listen.

You might be surprised to know that horses understand about seven to ten spoken words. I call them spoken words, rather than English words, because the people I know speak more than one language. I personally know nine words. But the really great thing is that I don't need a whole lot of words to communicate with people because I can interpret so many emotions. I get body language, too, and I always know kindness when I feel it. Basically, I understand much more than people think.

The specifics vary from horse to horse, but I personally understand all the following words when they are said aloud by people:

Walk

Trot

Canter

Whoa

Halt

Carrot

Good boy

Eddie

When you take the words that Melissa just said to Kennedy, for example, all I really got out of that was *trot*. So, I kept trotting. Melissa's voice also sounded kind and encouraging, which are good signs that I should continue what I'm doing; that I'm helping my rider learn.

I also know the meaning of two sounds that aren't technically words. I know that the clucking sound— when people suck down tight on their tongue and then release it—means to move forward. If I'm already moving forward, then the "cluck" means to go faster. (I've come to learn that people can mean more than one thing based on a single sound. It gets a little confusing.) I also know the sound of someone shaking my grain in a feed bucket, which means it's time to come into the barn to eat.

ALL of us know that sound, even from two paddocks away.

I feel pressure as my rider pulls on the reins, drawing the metal bit back into the corners of my mouth. I slow from a trot to a walk before I even hear Melissa say *whoa*.

"*Good boy, Eddie,*" she says with a laugh. Now that, I understood in its entirety. I love a *good boy, Eddie.*

We walk a lap around the ring before Kennedy steers me to the center. Melissa pats my head. Gallagher, one of the horses who gets turned out in the paddock with me, is also in the ring now. His lesson is about to start. We give each other a look, like a changing of the guard.

It's his turn now to take care of his rider. I love what I do, but I'm still a bit relieved when the lesson is done. It's hard work to keep a rider safe. Also, the end of the lesson means I get a nice brushing, and sometimes a carrot.

U

As I walk past Gallagher, I wish him good luck. Horses don't communicate out loud the way people do, but I can hear what other horses are telling me, and they can hear what I tell them, especially once we get to know each other. People don't pick up on this, of course. If they did, we'd all understand each other with a whole lot less fuss! Horses do "speak" to each other from time to time, but mostly it's just listening and feeling. If you ask me, I think people could probably benefit from less talking and more feeling.

Horses use our bodies, too, to show what we are thinking. People can usually decipher our body language, if they're paying attention. Pinned ears means we're angry, and ears perked forward means we're concentrating on something. One or both ears cocked gently back means we're listening.

It all seems much easier than the way people communicate.

Kennedy takes her feet out of the stirrups and swings one leg over the back of my saddle. Melissa is taking her through the steps of dismounting. Next, Kennedy slides down my left side, gripping the saddle with both hands as she allows her body to slink down to the ground. When her feet hit the dirt, she stumbles back a few steps as she regains her balance. I may not be very big for a horse, but it's a long way down when you're not very big for a person.

Kennedy gives me a big pat on my neck. It was a good first lesson. Melissa leads me out of the ring, and we walk outside on the way back to my stall. An evening breeze rustles the leaves on the trees all around us. I watch as a few of them float lazily to the ground.

I think I'm going to like this place.

CPSIA information can be obtained
at www.ICGtesting.com
Printed in the USA
JSHW031926290623
44021JS00005B/252